Guarding His Fortune

Stella Bagwell

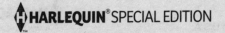

HARLEQUIN® SPECIAL EDITION

Special thanks and acknowledgment are given to
Stella Bagwell for her contribution to the
Fortunes of Texas: The Lost Fortunes series.

Recycling programs
for this product may
not exist in your area.

ISBN-13: 978-1-335-57376-6

Guarding His Fortune

Copyright © 2019 by Harlequin Books S.A.

HARLEQUIN®
www.Harlequin.com

Printed in U.S.A.

Chapter One

Savannah Fortune struggled to hide her impatience as she gazed toward the opposite end of the study where her father, Miles, was standing in front of a massive cherrywood desk. Tall and tanned, with short graying brown hair, he made an imposing figure in a gray suit and power-red tie. Next to him in a plush armchair, her mother, Sarah, dressed impeccably in a white dress and pearls, waited for her husband to address the family.

"This is ridiculous." Savannah's hushed voice was directed at her younger sister, Belle. "Why has Dad called this urgent meeting in the middle of the day? Couldn't he have waited until dinner this evening?"

Belle slanted her a droll look. "Urgent means he wants his children to focus on him. Not the boudin kolaches and gumbo we're having for supper."

Miles rapped his knuckles on the desktop and everyone in the room turned their attention to the patriarch of the New Orleans Fortunes.

"I'm glad to see everyone is here," he spoke, his strong voice reverberating around the room. "I'll try to make this as concise as possible."

A few steps away, Savannah's older brother, Austin, held up a hand. "Sorry to interrupt, Dad, but Nolan isn't here. Shouldn't he be privy to this family meeting, too?"

"Nolan has already been informed of everything I'm about to relay to all of you." Turning slightly, Miles picked up a large manila envelope from the desktop and held it up for his family to see. "Earlier this morning I received this detailed report and as much as I hate to alarm all of you, the news is jarring."

Jarring? Now that Savannah was taking closer notice, her father appeared drawn and pale. What was in that envelope? As far as she knew, Fortune Investments, her father's massive banking business, was as lucrative as ever.

Leaning closer to Belle, Savannah whispered in her sister's ear. "Has the stock market crashed or something?"

Belle made a hands-up gesture to say she didn't have a clue as to what might be going on. Across the room, their older sister, Georgia, was arching a questioning brow at their brother Beau. From the lost expressions on the faces of Savannah's siblings, it appeared all were a bit mystified by this meeting.

Miles cleared his throat and continued, "The news is conclusive. The Fortune family is being targeted."

This wasn't exactly breaking news, Savannah thought. Especially the kind that warranted a family meeting.

Apparently, her brother Draper was thinking along those same lines. He said, "I don't mean to sound like a snob, but being wealthy has always made us targets, Dad."

Miles nodded. "You couldn't be more correct, son. However, this situation is different. Someone is deliberately trying to harm members of the Fortune family. As you all know, there's already been an arson in Austin that came close to being deadly, a cyber-attack at Robinson Tech and a real-estate sabotage in Houston. We have no way of knowing who or what might be next. We do have reason to believe that Charlotte Robinson is behind all these incidents."

"Do you know this for certain?" Georgia asked. "It seems strange the woman would want to hurt her own children."

Miles pecked a finger against the manila envelope. "As you all have learned, my half brother Kenneth Fortunado in Houston has a son, Connor, who's a highly skilled private investigator. Connor has continued to dig up information about Charlotte and he's recently discovered the divorce between her and Gerald recently became final."

Austin quickly countered. "Why should we be concerned about this? We're not a part of the Austin Fortunes or the Houston Fortunes. Undoubtedly, we're related to them, but we've never even met most of them."

Austin's remarks matched the ones going through Savannah's head. The other Fortunes were strangers. In fact, only a few months had passed since Miles had admitted to his children that he was actually an illegitimate son of Julius Fortune, the man who'd also fathered Gerald Robinson aka Jerome Fortune. At that time, Miles had beseeched his children to keep the secret under wraps. However, it wasn't long afterward that the long-buried truth had somehow gotten back to the Austin Fortunes and from there it had spread.

Miles placed a protective hand on his wife's shoulder as he answered Austin's question. "Gerald and Charlotte were married for thirty-some years. Plenty of baggage and money has accrued over that length of time. The woman is furious that she's losing out. Not to mention that she's been humiliated in public by Gerald's endless philandering. Make no mistake, she's seeking vengeance on the Fortune family. And I'm very concerned the woman has most likely learned I am a half brother to her ex-husband, Gerald Robinson. And regrettably, that makes all of us an enemy in her eyes."

Everyone began to talk at once, bouncing questions and opinions back and forth until the room sounded like Bourbon Street during Mardi Gras. Savannah was content to stand to one side and wait for the commotion to die down. After all, she was soon going to be off on her own and away from the family. This Charlotte-threat didn't apply to her.

Eventually, Miles called for silence. "I'm due back at the office in half an hour, so I need to wrap up this meeting," he announced. "Are there any last questions before I leave?"

Belle asked a basic one. "So what does this mean for all of us, Dad?"

Miles somber gaze encompassed his whole family as he spoke. "It means all of us need to remain on high alert and be vigilant of people, our surroundings and anything out of the ordinary. Meanwhile, if any new information about Charlotte comes to me, it will be passed on to all of you."

He assisted Sarah from the chair and as their mother made her way out of the study, everyone followed, including Savannah, who was on the tail end of the group.

She was about to step into the hallway when Miles suddenly called to her. "Savannah, please remain in the study. I'd like a private word with you."

Smiling to herself, she made an abrupt about-face and walked back to the center of the room. Her father was going to congratulate her on being invited to the University of Texas to join an important study group, she thought. No doubt, he was proud to hear his daughter would be studying with one of the most elite professors in the field of epidemiology.

"Yes, Dad?"

He gestured for her to take a seat in the same chair her mother had occupied.

She shook her head. "I don't need to sit."

Actually, she was impatient to get back to her bedroom, where suitcases and garments were laid across every inch of the king-sized bed. By the end of the day, she wanted to have everything packed and ready for the move.

"Sit down anyway." He adjusted the knot of his tie, then placed the report about Charlotte Robinson into the leather briefcase he carried to work.

Biting back a sigh, Savannah eased into the chair nearest to her and smoothed the hem of her mint-green skirt over her knees.

"Okay, I'm sitting," she said cheerfully, then shot him a smug smile. "I assume Mother told you my good news."

Easing a hip onto the corner of the desk, he said flatly, "She told me. Unfortunately, that's why we're having this talk."

Instead of sounding like a preening father, his voice was crisp and resolute. It was the same unyielding tone she often heard him use on the phone with a business crony.

Frowning, she asked, "Dad, aren't you happy about the invitation?"

"I'm always proud of my children's achievements." His response was hardly encouraging. "Being invited to join a study group probably doesn't sound like much to you. But in my world, it's quite an honor."

He shook his head. "Savannah, I realize the invitation from the university is a big coup for you. And normally I'd be the first to give you a proud send-off to Austin. But considering all the troubles that have been plaguing the Fortunes, I have to insist that you cancel your trip to Texas."

Her jaw dropped. "Cancel? You must be joking! You don't just cancel an invitation to study with a group of brilliant graduate students and a professor who has an impressive reputation as being one of the best in his field. There are hundreds of students who'd kill to be in my position!"

"And there's one person out there who might literally want to kill you just because your name is Fortune," he shot back at her. "No, Savannah, I'm very serious about this. Austin is full of Fortunes. It's where Gerald's business, Robinson Tech, is located. Living there would place you in the thick of danger."

"But Nolan lives there," she argued. "If he can, then so can I."

Miles muttered something under his breath and Savannah knew better than to ask him to repeat it. Frankly, she'd never seen her father looking so stressed. Not even when the stock market took a wild plunge, or a huge investment had gone bankrupt.

"Nolan is a grown man with a family," he reasoned.

And being twenty-five and a single woman made her incapable of taking care of herself? She wanted to fling the question at her father. But she was smart enough to know that sparring with him in that manner would only send his blood pressure to the boiling point. Miles Fortune was old-school. Women of the family were to be pampered and protected. Men were expected to show strength and wisdom.

"I'm fully grown, too, Dad. And my career, my education are very important to me."

"Your life is more important to me," he retorted.

Frustration caused her head to swing back and forth. "But, Dad, I've already rented an apartment in Austin and purchased a plane ticket! I'm in the process of packing!"

"Sorry. Cancel everything. When this ordeal with Charlotte Robinson is over, then you may reschedule your studies."

Reschedule? By the time Charlotte Robinson was tracked down and punished for her misdeeds, Savannah wouldn't be able to fetch herself an invitation to a dogfight, much less to the university study!

She leaned toward him, her expression beseeching him to understand the importance of her trip to Austin. "Dad, you've been a businessman for the major part of your life. More than anyone, you understand that to get ahead you have to strike while the iron is hot. I have to jump at this study now! I won't have another chance like this."

His expression was unrelenting. "I won't have a daughter of mine running around on her own in Austin! You'd constantly be in the crosshairs! You might as well pin a sign to your back with the name *Fortune* written in bold letters."

"Dad, for heaven's sake, most of my waking hours will be spent at the university. I'm sure the security there will be more than adequate."

Before he could shoot a negative reply at her, Savannah rose from the chair and started out of the study.

"Savannah, I'm serious about this. You're not going."

Glancing over her shoulder, she smiled at him. "This

is my life. My career. I am going, Dad. And I hope it will be with your blessings."

"That isn't going to happen, young lady!"

Her chin high, Savannah walked through the door, then carefully closed it behind her.

Living in New Orleans all her life, Savannah was long accustomed to hot, steamy weather, even for the first day of April, so when she stepped through the glass doors of Austin-Bergstrom International Airport, the oppressive afternoon heat hardly caught her attention. But a man walking straight in her direction had definitely caught her attention. Somewhere near thirty, he was at least six foot three or four with enough muscles to suggest he spent hours in the gym. His tanned complexion and black close-cropped hair coupled with a neatly trimmed goatee and mustache conjured up an image of dark and deliciously dangerous.

And the danger grew even closer as he stopped a few steps in front of her. "Miss Fortune?"

She instinctively glanced around the busy entrance to make sure the dreamy hunk of a man wasn't address-ing someone else. "That's right," she finally answered. "How did you guess?"

A faint, almost cocky grin lifted a corner of his mas-culine lips and for a brief moment, Savannah couldn't tear her eyes away from the sexy sight of straight white teeth, an unyielding jaw and chocolate-brown eyes fringed with thick black lashes.

"I'm Chaz Mendoza and it's my job to be a good guesser." He gestured to a sleek black car parked at the curbside of the sheltered portico. "I'm here to take you to your destination. Are those your bags?"

The question snapped her out of her survey of his

chiseled features, and she glanced over her left shoulder to where a valet was pushing a cart loaded with the luggage she'd just collected from the baggage carousel. "Those are all mine."

Before she could ask him if the university had sent a car to collect her, the man was already directing the baggage attendant to the trunk of the waiting car.

Standing to one side, Savannah allowed her gaze to wander discreetly over the driver. The navy short-sleeved polo shirt and tight jeans he was wearing showed off every hard muscle of his brawny physique. Everything about him exuded authority and strength.

Chaz Mendoza. The name sounded very familiar, but try as she might, she couldn't recall exactly where she might have heard it. And she knew for certain she'd never met him before. He was the type of man a woman didn't forget.

Oh, well, she thought, he was hardly any business of hers and she'd not traveled all the way to Austin to have her focus derailed by a man. Even if he was scrumptious eye candy.

He slammed the trunk shut on her baggage and the sound pushed her out of her musings. She quickly opened her handbag and handed several bills to the valet.

The lanky young man thanked her with an appreciative grin, then hurried off with the empty cart.

Savannah looked at the driver. "I was expecting to catch a taxi to my apartment. This is certainly nice of the university to provide me with a ride. Funny, though. I don't recall giving anyone the arrival time of my flight."

"It probably just slipped your mind. I think right now, we'd better be on our way. This parking spot is limited to a few minutes." He cupped a hand beneath her elbow and escorted her around to the passenger side of the car.

After he'd helped her into the plush bucket seat and joined her in the car, Savannah gave him the address of her new apartment.

"If the address isn't recognizable to you, I have a navigation map on my phone," she offered as she snapped the seat belt in place.

He quickly belted himself in and merged the car into the slow moving line of traffic exiting the airport. "Thank you, but my car is equipped with a navigational system. I'm familiar with that particular part of the city anyway."

"Oh, that's good," she told him. "I hope I'll soon learn my way around. Of course, I need to pick up a car of my own before I start trying to navigate the city streets."

He glanced in her direction and Savannah found herself looking directly into his brown eyes. The connection rattled her for a brief moment before she purposely turned her attention to the traffic in front of them.

"So you're not familiar with Austin?" he asked.

His voice was slow, and warm, and just rough enough to cause goose bumps to rise along the back of her arms. Or was that the cold air blowing from the vents on the car dash? Either way, her reaction to the man was making her feel more than foolish.

She took a deep breath and blew it out. "No. I'm from New Orleans."

From the corner of her eye, she could see a faint smile touch his lips. "So that's where that lilting drawl of yours comes from."

"And yours doesn't exactly sound Texan. Are you a native Austinite?"

"No. My family is originally from Florida, but in the past several years most of them, including me, have migrated here to Texas."

"I see. So you and your family obviously like it here," she said.

"Very much."

Savannah sighed as thoughts of her father once again drifted through her mind. Since the day of the family meeting, she'd expected him to be fighting her tooth and nail over this Austin trip. Instead, he'd avoided her completely. Even this morning, before she left the Fortune mansion to catch her flight, she expected him to give her a few parting words of warning. Instead, her mother had informed her that Miles had skipped breakfast to make an early downtown business meeting. So much for worrying about her safety, she thought glumly, much less wishing her good luck.

"Is anything wrong?" her driver asked.

Was her state of mind so transparent that a stranger could read her troubled thoughts? She darted a glance at him.

"No. Everything is fine," she said. "I'll just be glad to get to my apartment. I've never really cared for flying. Once I'm back on solid ground, I always feel drained."

"Have you done much of it? Flying, that is."

From the corner of her eye, she could see his left hand resting comfortably on the steering wheel. There was no sign of a wedding band and the fact that she was even bothering to look caused a tinge of embarrassment to warm her cheeks.

What are you thinking, Savannah? Take a closer gander at this guy. You think he got those muscles from relaxing in a recliner in front of the TV? This man is as far from married as a man can get.

Clearing her throat, she pulled her straying thoughts back to his question. "I've flown across country many times, and overseas. I see it as a necessary evil to get to where I'm going. What about you? Do you travel much?"

"I used to. But not since I've moved to Austin. I guess you could say I've already gotten to where I'm going."

She smiled at him. "Hmm. That must be nice. To know that you're in the right place and exactly where you belong."

By now, they were traveling a busy highway that led deeper into the city. If Savannah had taken a taxi as she'd originally planned, she would've been taking note of her surroundings and the city skyline ahead of them. But Chaz Mendoza's huge masculine presence was distracting her from seeing Austin clearly for the first time.

"Is that why you've come to Texas? To figure out where you belong?"

It was a rather personal question to be posed by a stranger, she thought. Especially one who'd been hired to simply drive her from the airport to her apartment. But to be fair, she hadn't exactly been discussing the weather with him.

"Not really. I know my roots are in New Orleans. I'm here because I've been invited to partake in a study group at the university for a few weeks."

"That sounds very impressive."

At least someone thinks so, Savannah thought. "I feel honored to be included. It's something I've been wanting and working toward for a long time."

"What are you studying?"

"Epidemiology."

"Sorry, you'll have to explain that a bit more. I'm not a science person."

She wanted to ask what kind of person he was, but quickly decided that would be too obvious. The last thing she wanted this man to think was that she was flirting with him. For heaven's sake, she didn't flirt with anyone. It wasn't her nature. Besides, she didn't have time for such nonsense.

"Don't feel badly. Most people aren't familiar with the word. It's a study of diseases. Why people get them and what we can do to prevent them—as in finding the biggest risk factors. There are different fields to study in epidemiology. For instance how certain diseases affect society and the workplace and the cost of caring for such illnesses."

"And what field are you focusing on?"

No doubt, he was asking just to make polite conversation, Savannah decided. Most men around her age were turned off by the subject. He might be truly interested if she were discussing quarterbacks in the NFL, or point guards in the NBA, but not medical science.

"I'm concentrating on the branch that studies why people get diseases and certain illnesses and what we can do to prevent them."

"An admirable profession, I'd say."

"I like to think so. My studies—" She broke off as she realized she was about to say her studies consumed her life. For some reason she didn't want this sexy man to think she was little more than a brain in a white lab coat. "They're very important to me. So that's why I'm here in Austin."

He glanced in her direction and Savannah got the strange impression he was something more than just a driver for the university. The notion shook her, until he smiled and then suddenly everything felt right again.

"Well, welcome to Texas, Miss Fortune. I hope you enjoy your time here."

"Thanks. I hope I do, too."

This was going to be much harder than he'd ever anticipated, Chaz decided, as he braked the car to a stop in front of the luxurious gated apartment building where Miss Savannah Fortune would be living until she finished her stint at the university.

Obviously, her father had told her nothing about hiring a bodyguard to protect her while she was here in Austin. And Chaz had yet to find the right moment to tell her exactly why he'd intercepted her at the airport.

If she'd hadn't looked so damned beautiful when he spotted her emerging through the doors of the terminal, his brain might have remained focused on his job. And if she hadn't been so open and warm when he'd introduced himself, he might've been able to come right out and inform her that he was working for her father.

But the sight of Savannah had thrown him for a loop. She'd scarcely resembled the foggy pic Miles Fortune had texted him earlier this morning. It was a good thing the man had warned Chaz she'd be dressed in a cream-colored pencil skirt and a pale pink blouse; otherwise, he would've missed her entirely.

Damn the man! When Miles Fortune had first contacted Chaz about providing security for his daughter, he'd described Savannah as the studious sort, who rarely took her nose out of a book. According to him, she had a very limited social life and made a point of avoiding men entirely. She'd be easy to keep an eye on, Miles had told him.

Hell, the man was either blind or knew very little about his own child, Chaz thought with a heavy dose of frustration. Keeping his eyes on Savannah Fortune was going to be easy. It was keeping his hands off her for the next few weeks that was going to pose the problem.

Chaz had assumed he was going to be guarding a meek young woman, whose idea of an exciting evening was to watch an educational channel on TV. This young beauty looked as though she'd be very much at home on the dance floor and in the arms of a very attentive man.

Trying not to dwell on that image, he peered across the narrow console to see she was leaning slightly forward, peering through the windshield at the entrance of the apartment. The movement caused a long curtain of smooth brown hair to slip forward and partially hide her face. Chaz wanted to reach over and tuck the silky strands behind her ear. Not because he needed to see her lovely features. No, the image of her face was already burned into his brain. He simply wanted to touch her and discover for himself if she felt as soft and womanly as she actually looked.

"That's the correct number," she stated happily. "And the outside certainly looks pretty."

Chaz pulled his gaze away from her long enough to study the entrance to the redbrick apartment. A dark green door with a brass knocker was shaded by the overhang of a square concrete porch. On one corner, a huge planter spilled over with red and pink geraniums.

The apartment was definitely not typical budget-friendly housing, he decided. It was for the elite class and more like a fancy townhouse than an apartment. But then, he'd not expected anything less from a Fortune.

"I'd say it appears to be exceptionally nice. Did you rent it sight unseen?"

She nodded. "Live Oak Lane is supposed to be one of the best gated communities in Austin and I studied photos on their website before I signed the lease. But sometimes pics can be doctored. I'm hoping that's not the case when I see the inside of the apartment." She unlatched her seat belt and pulled the strap of an expensive leather handbag over her shoulder. "If you'll be kind enough to help me get my bags to the door, I'll let you be on your way."

"My pleasure," he murmured.

After pushing a button to release the trunk, he skirted the hood to help her out of the car. When she placed her little hand in his, Chaz was instantly swamped with all sorts of protective feelings. Most of which had nothing to do with his job.

Once she was standing next to him on the concrete drive, she looked up at him and smiled and though he was cursing at himself to step back and wedge a respectable amount of distance between them, all he could do was hold on to her fingers and stare into her hazel eyes. Green, blue or brown, he wasn't sure which color was dominant, but he was quite certain he'd never seen anything so sparkly or full of life.

"Thank you, Chaz."

"You're entirely welcome, Miss Fortune."

Clearing his throat, he forced himself to drop her hand and turn to the task of lifting her bags from the trunk. As soon as he had them on the ground, she grabbed up a floral tote and a midsized suitcase with wheels.

"I can manage these two," she said and headed to the entrance of the apartment.

As Chaz followed with two bags stuffed under each arm, he glanced furtively around the apartment complex. There were five tenants to the right of Savannah's flat, four to the left and no second floors to any of them. At least that was a plus for security, he thought. But the beautiful landscaping separating the lawns of each apartment could create a nightmare if anyone decided to hide behind the giant blooming oleanders or bushes of Texas sage.

When he reached the door, Savannah was already digging through her handbag for the key.

"Just put them anywhere," she told him. "I'll get them inside."

He set the bags down and took a deep breath. His time had run out, he decided. There was no more delaying the inevitable.

"Uh—Miss Fortune, I think—"

Before he could push the remaining words past his lips, she smiled and offered him her hand in a gesture of farewell.

"I know what you're going to say. It was nice meeting this way."

"It couldn't have been nicer," he agreed, while thinking he could stand here holding on to her hand for hours and never get tired of looking at her plush lips, or short little nose, or those luminous eyes fringed by the longest lashes he'd ever seen.

"Perhaps I'll see you around campus sometime," she said. "But then, I suppose you're always busy carting people to and fro."

He tried not to wince at the deduction he'd allowed her to make of him. "Actually, Miss Fortune, you're going to be seeing quite a bit of me."

Her eyes suddenly wary, she purposely pulled her hand from his. "Oh? I don't understand."

"I'm sorry. I should have explained the moment I introduced myself at the airport. But I…thought it might be nicer if the two of us got to know each other a bit before I sprang the situation on you."

She was shaking her head now and Chaz saw a look of confusion and something close to fear fill her eyes.

"Situation? What are you talking about?"

"My name is Chaz Mendoza, but the university didn't send me to collect you at the airport. Your father did."

She took a step backward. "Excuse me?"

"Your father is Miles Fortune of Fortune Investments in New Orleans, right?"

Although her nod was an affirmative, her eyes were glazed with shock. "Yes, he is my father. But why—"

Before she could question him further, he said, "He's hired me as your bodyguard, Miss Fortune."

She gasped with disbelief. "Bodyguard! You must be joking!"

"Hardly. I don't joke about providing security. From what Mr. Fortune tells me, you could be putting yourself in quite a bit of danger. My job is to see that danger doesn't get anywhere near you."

So this was why her father hadn't spoken to her before she'd departed New Orleans, she thought. He'd believed he'd taken control of the situation by hiring her a bodyguard.

"This is incredible! I can't believe my father would go so far as to—" Her gaze swept over him as though she were seeing him for the first time today and then her head began to swing back and forth. "Hire a man to follow me around! It won't work. It simply won't work. As of this moment, you can consider yourself relieved of your duties."

During the brief ride over from the airport, Chaz had made the mistake of thinking she was different from the wealthy people who often visited his family's businesses, Mendoza Winery and La Viña restaurant. As they'd made conversation, she'd not come across as a spoiled little rich girl. But she was certainly coming across as one now.

"Sorry. You didn't hire me, Miss Fortune. So you can hardly terminate my services."

To underscore the fact that he wasn't going anywhere,

Chaz pulled a key from his jeans pocket and unlocked the door.

Her mouth fell open. "Where did you get that key?" she demanded. "And don't tell me you're planning on staying here! In *my* apartment!"

Smiling smugly, he pushed the door open and gestured for her to precede him into the building.

"Don't worry about how I got a key. And don't be thinking you can run to the building manager and complain. Your father has already taken care of everything."

"That's what he thinks! There's no way in hell I'm going to share my living space with a man!"

Her plush lips flattened to an angry line as she brushed past him, but Chaz was paying very little attention to her outrage as she marched ahead of him. No, he was much more focused on the sweet flowery scent of her perfume and the evocative sway of her round little bottom.

"Don't worry, Miss Fortune. You'll get used to me."

Looking over her shoulder, she glared at him. "Never!"

Something about her ruffled feathers made her even more attractive than when she'd been making polite conversation and Chaz couldn't stop himself from smiling at her.

"Never say never, Miss Fortune. It might come back to haunt you."

She stomped out of the foyer and as Chaz followed after her, he realized his job as a bodyguard had just taken on a new meaning.

Chapter Two

Savannah hardly noticed the plush furnishings of the living room or the beautiful bay window overlooking a landscaped walking path on the opposite side of the street. At the moment, she couldn't have cared less about her surroundings. She was more than angry. She was in panic mode.

Dropping the bags she'd been carrying onto the hardwood floor, she plucked her cell phone from her handbag and punched in her father's private number.

As she waited for him to answer, she heard Chaz Mendoza's footsteps entering the room. A second later, he walked past her and she watched him place her suitcases near a doorway leading out of the spacious living area.

She was trying to pull her gaze off his bulging biceps when her father's voice suddenly sounded in her ear.

"Hello, Savannah. I'm assuming that you've landed safely in Austin and have met Mr. Mendoza."

Savannah wanted to yell at him. But the anger coursing through her was not enough to override the respect she'd always shown her mother and her father.

Shoving out a long pent-up breath, she unconsciously gravitated toward the window. "Yes, I'm safely here in Austin. At my apartment. I'm calling because I want to know what you were thinking, Dad. I can't have a body-guard tagging along after me! Not only would it be em-barrassing, it's impractical, illogical and—"

"And very necessary, Savannah."

Savannah never cursed, but she found herself having to bite down on her tongue to keep from spouting a few choice words into the phone.

"Necessary? I hardly think so, Dad! My time here is going to be very low-key. How—"

"Low-key or not, I want Chaz with you. And no amount of arguing or pleading is going to change my mind, Savannah."

"But, Dad, I can't—"

"Look, Savannah, you are the one who went ahead with this trip in spite of my disapproval. You want to be independent? Then act grown up and accept that having protection close by is a smart thing, not an encumbrance."

For the past four years, ever since Savannah had turned twenty-one, she'd wanted her parents to see her as a self-sufficient adult, a smart woman who could handle the daily problems that life threw at her. Since then, she'd acquired her bachelor degree and moved on to her grad-uate studies. Yet, in spite of those hard-earned achieve-ments, her father believed she still had a lot to learn.

She drew in a deep breath and blew it out, while from the corner of her right eye she watched Chaz come to stand at the opposite end of the large window. He was either taking in the view or listening in on her conversa-tion, she thought crossly.

"Dad, I want my privacy. It's essential that my studies not be distracted—"

"I'm positive that you and Mr. Mendoza will work out some type of house rules to suit your needs."

House rules! She wanted to ask him how he'd like some stranger creeping through the house while he tried to focus on his work. Instead, she said, "Listen, Dad, I'm going to tell Mr. Mendoza that his services aren't needed. I—"

"I'm the only person who can fire the guy," Miles bluntly interrupted. "And right now, I have no intentions of doing such a thing. So make the most of your time there, Savannah. It could end sooner than you think."

She started to ask him what he meant by that remark when the doorbell suddenly rang. Completely exasperated, she said, "There's someone at the door, Dad. We'll talk about this again. Soon!"

By the time she ended the call, Chaz had already left his spot at the window to go answer the door. Savannah followed, while trying to imagine who at the university might've taken it upon themselves to visit her today.

As she turned the corner leading into the foyer, she could see Chaz pushing the door wide and her brother Nolan stepping over the threshold. Since he was dressed in a business suit, Savannah assumed he'd taken a break from work to see her. But why? He could've waited until tonight, or any opportune time to welcome her to Austin.

"Hello, Chaz," her brother greeted the bodyguard. "Nice to see you again."

The two men finished shaking hands and from the easy way they greeted each other, it was obvious they'd met before. Which only proved that Nolan had to be in on this whole bodyguard matter.

Just great, she thought angrily. Her family was ganging up on her.

Spotting her, Nolan moved away from Chaz and walked over to where she stood at the end of the foyer. A wide smile creased his handsome face. "Hi, sis."

"What are you doing here?" she asked bluntly.

"Wow! That has to be one of the nicest greetings I've ever received," he joked. "Especially from my little sister."

"I'm not exactly feeling nice." She glanced at Chaz to see he was busy bolting the door behind him. Apparently, security was always on his mind.

"I assume you're not happy about Dad supplying you with a bodyguard."

She rolled her eyes. "How would you feel about someone invading your privacy? I was so looking forward to this time here in Austin and now I—"

Nolan held up a hand. "Whoa, sis! Just a minute. I think we need to talk this out calmly and rationally."

Savannah drew in a deep breath and blew it out. "I am calm! Or at least I will be as soon as you tell Mr. Mendoza his services aren't needed."

His expression stoic, Chaz strolled up to them. "I don't think your sister understands the risk she'd be taking by running around Austin on her own," he said to Nolan. "Maybe if you explained it to her, she might realize I'm a friend, not a foe."

"I think you're right," Nolan said to him, then wrapping a hand around Savannah's upper arm, urged her out of the foyer. "Come on, sis, let's go sit down and talk about this."

"I don't want to sit. I don't want to talk. I want to be alone! Can't you, or Dad, or—" she turned a glare on Chaz Mendoza "—or you understand that?"

"I do understand. More than you think." Nolan shook his head. "This isn't how you pictured your stay here in Austin. But since you received the invitation from UT, our family situation has changed."

In the living room, Savannah allowed Nolan to lead her over to a beige leather couch. As she took a seat close to her brother's side, Chaz eased into a matching armchair directly across from them. Obviously, he had no intention of allowing her to have a private conversation with her own brother, she thought crossly.

Doing her best to ignore Chaz's huge presence, she said to Nolan, "I haven't noticed anything changing with our family. It's the *other* Fortunes who are having problems. We're not a part of them. We never have been."

Nolan let out a weary sigh, while Chaz appeared unfazed by her protest. No doubt, both of them thought she was behaving in a childish fashion, Savannah thought. But at the moment, she didn't care. This was her life. And she had a right to live it *her* way. Not the way her father wanted or expected.

"Nolan, contrary to what Dad might think of me, I am a grown woman. I know how to take care of myself," she argued. "It's not like anyone has been threatening me personally. Or even stalking me. Just because I happen to have Fortune for a last name doesn't mean I'm in some sort of dire danger."

As soon as her words died away, Chaz spoke. "Your father seems to think so."

Nolan quickly supported Chaz's claim. "That's right, Savannah. Dad is very concerned. Not only about you, but about the entire family."

Unconvinced, Savannah looked at her brother. "And what about you, Nolan? Are you concerned that Lizzie and little Stella might be in danger? Have you hired a bodyguard for them, or yourself?"

"Not yet. But I'm seriously thinking about it. Your situation is entirely different, though. My wife and child aren't alone. They have me."

And Savannah now had Chaz. So according to Nolan, and her father, that fixed everything. The idea had Savannah groaning out loud.

"To me, this all seems blown out of proportion. Why would a crazy ex-wife of Gerald Robinson have anything against me? She doesn't even know me. Besides, has anyone really proved that these unfortunate occurrences are connected to her?"

"I'm not sure if there's enough proof for a prosecutor to convict her in court," Nolan answered. "At least, not yet. But Connor Fortunado has managed to connect enough dots to tell us that she's the one behind these criminal incidents. And the mere fact that she's been digging into our family background should be enough to scare you into wanting a bodyguard."

Maybe. But the thought of being in close proximity with Chaz on a daily basis was just as scary. She was a cerebral person and that was the sort of man she'd always been attracted to—the sort that would be compatible with her life. Even so, just looking at Chaz set her nerves on edge and pushed her pulse to an unhealthy rate. Her reaction to the man was silly and there was no way she could admit such a thing to her brother. She didn't even want to admit it to herself.

"When an evil person is out for revenge, he or she will usually start with the easiest, most vulnerable target. And I'd put you in that category, Miss Fortune," Chaz said.

"Chaz is one hundred percent right," Nolan agreed. "And surely you've not forgotten what happened here in Austin earlier this year, Savannah. We were attending Schuyler Fortunado's family reunion party when the fire broke out at Gerald Robinson's estate. Ben was seriously injured."

How could Savannah have forgotten the reunion? In spite of their parents choosing to stay behind in New Orleans, she and her six siblings had decided to attend. All seven of them had traveled to Austin, believing they'd be meeting many of the Fortune family, particularly Gerald Robinson's children, who were theoretically cousins to Savannah and her siblings. Yet, none of that branch of the family had shown at the party that night. Not until Olivia had come bursting in with the shocking news that a fire had broken out at the Robinson estate.

"No. I've not forgotten. After the fire, we all went over and helped as much as we could with the cleanup." The memory of that chilling incident caused some of the anger to drain out of her. "Everyone feared that Ben was going to die from the injuries he'd sustained in the fire."

"It's a miracle he didn't," Nolan replied.

As the details of that night replayed in Savannah's mind, another thought suddenly struck her. One that should have registered with her the moment Chaz had introduced himself at the airport.

She turned a curious look on Chaz. "If I remember correctly, Schuyler married a man by the name of Mendoza. Carlo Mendoza, I think. The reunion was held at a winery by the same name and some of his family were in attendance that night. Are those your relations?"

He inclined his dark head. "That's right. Carlo is my brother. My family owns and operates the Mendoza Winery."

"And the La Viña restaurant. Which, by the way, serves delicious food," Nolan spoke up. "Maybe you can talk Chaz into taking you there some evening. Trust me, sis, it would be a treat."

A treat? Savannah stared at her brother, while wondering what he could possibly be thinking to suggest such a thing. In the first place, Savannah rarely went out on dates. Period. And even if she did decide to have dinner with a man, it certainly wouldn't be with Chaz Mendoza. He was a bodyguard! A big hunk of muscles with a dazzling smile. He wasn't her type at all!

Rising to her feet, Savannah began to move restlessly around the room. Learning that Chaz was her cousin Schuyler's brother-in-law made things even more awkward. Had her father been aware that Chaz had a connection to the Fortune family? Was that why he'd hired him to be her bodyguard?

"There's a troubled frown on your face, Savannah," Nolan remarked after a moment. "And it doesn't look good on you."

She paused to glance at her brother. "Exactly why are you here? Dad send you to bolster his case?"

Nolan grimaced, then made a palms up gesture with both hands. "Dad figured you were probably going to give Chaz a few problems. And he wanted me to be here to point out the reasons you need to have a bodyguard around."

Her father had definitely figured right, Savannah thought. For a number of reasons, many of which she didn't want to examine, she wanted to usher Chaz right out the door and out of her life.

"Okay, so there was a fire and Ben was injured," she said. "I'll concede that much. But—"

"And there was cyber hacking at Robinson Tech, along with the sabotage on the Fortunado Real Estate business," Nolan interrupted. "That should remind you that an evil

mind is out to destroy the Fortune family. And with Charlotte reportedly digging into our family in New Orleans
that could only mean one thing. We're next on her radar."

As Savannah's gaze vacillated between the two grim-
faced men, she realized there was no way she could win
this argument. At least, not on this first day in the city.
But that didn't mean she was going to cave-in completely.
After she was here a few days, safely going about her
business, she could surely make her father and Chaz see
that having a bodyguard was overkill.

Releasing a long, weary breath, she returned to the
couch and sank down next to her brother. "Okay. I'm not
happy about this situation," she said grudgingly. "But to
keep Dad happy I suppose I can go along with it—for
a while."

Her concession put a look of immense relief on her
brother's face. "I assured Dad that you were far too intelligent to put up much of a fuss. Thanks for proving me
right."

Intelligent? Not hardly. At this very moment, she could
hardly dare herself to glance in Chaz's direction. She
didn't like the way the sight of him caused her breath to
catch in her throat. But hopefully she'd get used to him
and his big masculine presence and he'd be no more of
a distraction than a sleeping cat.

Sure, she thought wryly. Like she'd pay no attention
at all to a sleeping tiger.

Nolan pushed back the cuff of his white shirt to glance
at his watch. "Now that we have that settled I can spare
a few more minutes. Why don't we all have a cup of coffee or something?"

"Sorry. I'd be glad to offer you and Mr. Mendoza
something to drink, but I'm afraid I've not had time to

stock the apartment with food. Or anything else for that matter."

Nolan's expression was incredulous. "Savannah! I realize you've never lived away from home before—other than extended vacations. And we both know that you've never dealt with household or kitchen duties. But you should've already hired someone to furnish the apartment with everything. Groceries, linens—all the necessities. Are you expecting maid service to come in and do everything for you?"

Damn it! He was making her sound like some sort of pampered princess who didn't have enough sense to get out of the rain, Savannah thought. Wondering what Chaz could possibly be thinking about her, she glanced at him.

As her gaze clashed with his, he didn't hold back in expressing his thoughts on the subject.

He said, "If you're planning on hiring help, then I'll have to do a thorough background check before the person arrives. And the maid service will need to supply several legitimate references. I can't take a chance that someone with ill intent might try to gain access to your apartment by posing as a maid or house servant."

"Oh, for goodness' sakes, you two are making this whole thing sound like a scene from a spy movie!" she exclaimed. "And anyway, you're both wasting your breath. I'm not hiring maid service. I'll be doing everything for myself. And that includes going shopping for everything I need."

Nolan let out a scoffing laugh. "My little sister in a grocery store? That'll be a first!"

Savannah glared at him. "What would you know about it? You've not lived at home in ages. You have no idea if I go into food markets or discount stores."

He smothered a laugh behind his hand. "Sure, Savan-

nah. That skirt and blouse look like you grabbed them
straight off a discount rack. And those heels—I'll bet
you found those in a clearance bin."

She wasn't sure if it was anger at her brother or being
embarrassed in front of Chaz that was causing a wave of
heat to sweep across her face. One way or the other, she
didn't have to look in a mirror to know her cheeks were
pink. And why? Being wealthy or privileged wasn't a
crime, or anything to feel ashamed about.

"You're being obnoxious. You know for a fact that I've
never wanted or expected to be pampered. I've worked
hard to—"

Holding up both hands to halt her tirade, Nolan said,
"Hold on, sis. I was only teasing you. Geez, you need to
lighten up a bit."

A long sigh slipped out of her. "Sorry, Nolan, but this
has not been an easy day."

He must have recognized just how stressed she'd been
because he wrapped a comforting arm around her shoulders. "No, I'm the one who should be sorry, Savannah.
This was supposed to be a happy, special day for you. Instead, you're faced with learning you now have to share
your life with a bodyguard. I understand it's not easy.
But I'm sure Chaz is going to be as discreet as possible."

No matter if the man never said a word to her. No matter if he always did his best to keep a measurable distance between them. She would feel his presence. She
would *know* he was nearby watching her with those dark
brown eyes. The very thought made her inwardly shiver.

Forcing herself to look at him, she said, "I'm sorry,
Chaz. I don't have anything against you personally. How
could I? I don't even know you. I'm just more than a little
aggravated at my father for springing this on me. It was
an underhanded thing to do to me and to you."

"Me?" he asked, a puzzled frown marring his forehead.

"Yes. For putting you in such an awkward situation."

One of his big shoulders shrugged in a nonchalant way. "Don't worry about me, Miss Fortune. In my line of work, I can't worry about my feelings being hurt. And I don't need my ego stroked. The fact that you don't want a bodyguard is insignificant to me. Miles Fortune is the person who hired me. I'm working to please him. Not you."

Well, he'd made that plain enough. And though his feelings toward her shouldn't matter, she felt downright deflated.

Nolan awkwardly cleared his throat. "Okay, I can see my presence is no longer needed so I think it's time I head on back to work."

Her brother's announcement sent a rush of panic through Savannah. She quickly jumped to her feet and snatched a hold on his arm.

"I'll show you to the door," she said.

Without glancing in Chaz's direction, she practically jerked Nolan out of the living room and down the foyer to the front door.

"Savannah, you hardly need to play the hostess with me," Nolan said as she continued to cling to his arm.

"I'm not being a hostess. I'm being a sister," she said in a hushed tone, then motioned her head toward the living room. "I want you to tell me how I'm supposed to deal with this? With him?"

To her disbelief, Nolan grinned at her. "Savannah, you're an attractive young woman. Surely you know how to deal with a man."

Deal with a man like Chaz? The men she'd spent any kind of company with had all possessed mushroom complexions from spending all their time indoors. Their mus-

cles were softer than hers, and the gleam in their eye was
usually caused by a glare of light on their glasses.

"I can see you're not going to be any help at all."

Chuckling, he gently patted her cheek. "You're worrying way too much, Savannah. Just relax and enjoy having a strong man around to take care of you. You might
actually like it. In the meantime, call me or Lizzie if
you need us."

Nolan was making light of the whole situation and
Savannah supposed she should, too. Otherwise, she was
going to wind up looking like a frantic little mouse who
should've never left home.

Doing her best to smile, she leaned forward and kissed
his cheek. "You're right. I don't have a thing to worry
about. Except making a good impression at the university."

"And I have no doubt you'll do just that," he said as
he opened the door and stepped onto the porch. "See
you later, sis."

With a little wave, he strode off down the driveway.
Savannah watched him slide behind the wheel of his car
and drive away before she finally shut the door and engaged the dead bolt. The last thing she needed right now
was to get a lecture from Chaz about leaving the apartment unlocked, she thought.

When she returned to the living room, Chaz was gone,
so she walked straight to the kitchen. To her delight, the
room was equipped with beautiful oak cabinets with glass
doors. A work island with an inlaid cutting board, along
with a large indoor grill, was located in the middle of the
room. The appliances were stainless steel and very up to
date. Above the deep double-sink, a wide window over-
looked a small backyard with a brick patio, where a group
of red motel furniture was shaded by a massive live oak.

At least if she started feeling too suffocated by Chaz's presence, she could escape to the patio.

"Your brother is gone?"

The sound of Chaz's voice had her turning away from the window. "Yes. I think he'd had all of me he could take for one day."

He moved into the room and Savannah noticed he moved quietly, with the grace of an athlete. "It's obvious he's very fond of you. Have you two always been close?"

Telling herself to relax, she walked over to the island and ran her hand lightly over the cutting board. "I'm close to all my siblings. I'm not sure what my father has told you about our family, but there are seven of us children. I have four brothers and two sisters."

"And they all live in New Orleans, except for you and Nolan?"

She nodded. "That's right. He and his wife, Lizzie, married last March. They have a baby girl, Stella. Lizzie is from Austin and since Nolan is a jazz musician, he loves it here. And me—well, you already know why I'm here."

"Yes. To study."

He made it sound as though she were causing a great deal of problems over something she could be doing safely back in New Orleans. Or was she being overly defensive? Since she'd only met Chaz a little more than an hour ago, she couldn't assume what was going on in his head. He might not be thinking anything of the sort. After all, during their ride from the airport, he'd called her studies admirable. She'd felt certain his compliment was sincere. Now she wasn't sure about that or anything else.

Oh, God, she had to get a grip, she thought. Her mind was jumping in all sorts of directions and the last thing she wanted was for this man to think she was scatter-brained and unable to take care of herself.

"Well," she said with the most positive tone she could muster. "I'm going to deal with my bags and have a look at the rest of the apartment."

"Um, I think you should know that I've already put my things in the smaller bedroom. But if you prefer it over the larger one, I can easily move everything."

He'd already moved in? Before she'd even had a chance to see her own apartment? Oh, her father was definitely going to hear about this, she promised herself. But to keep the peace for now, she was going to do her best to get along with Chaz Mendoza.

"I appreciate your offer, but I'm sure the room will suit me."

One of his black brows arched as though he were surprised she was being agreeable, for once.

"Fine. I'll help you carry your bags," he said.

"Thank you. I'd appreciate that."

They started out of the kitchen and Chaz said, "The apartment is actually large for one person. Are you planning on entertaining friends while you're here?"

Did he mean friends in general, or men? Did she look like a party girl to him? She supposed it didn't matter, but the question left her a bit uncomfortable.

"Don't worry," she replied. "I have no plans to do any entertaining. Other than Nolan and his family, I don't know anyone here in Austin. If I invite anyone over, it will be them."

They entered the living room and Savannah paused to take a closer survey of the space. Besides the leather sofa and matching armchair, there was a platform rocker and footstool done in a knobby burgundy fabric. At the far end of the room, a large flat-screen TV sat atop an oak entertainment center. A remote for it was lying on the end of a long glass-topped coffee table.

She rarely watched television and had no plans to change her habits, but perhaps Chaz might enjoy the diversion, she thought.

He walked over to the window and peered out at the small front lawn. Savannah got the feeling he was studying more than the perfectly manicured St. Augustine grass and blooming oleanders. Did he really believe that Charlotte Robinson or her paid cronies would actually try to cause her harm? The idea seemed fantastic.

He said, "I'm sure you'll be making new friends at the university. If you do decide to have company, or a dinner party, be sure and tell me about it beforehand. I'll have to—"

"Do background checks on my guests?" she interrupted.

He walked over to where she was standing. "Maybe. Maybe not. I just need to be prepared. It's a part of my job—to keep you safe."

"Yes. By all means, I'll tell you every move I intend to make."

His gaze slipped over her face and for a moment Savannah was totally disarmed by his chocolate-brown eyes. As a bodyguard, she would've expected his gaze to be razor sharp. Instead, his eyes were soft and alluring. And it suddenly dawned on Savannah that if she weren't careful, she might easily get lost in those deep, dark pools.

"I'm sorry you're so displeased about this," he said. "But one day you might be very thankful your father was so concerned about you."

She couldn't imagine herself being thankful for having her stay in Austin invaded by this man. But she didn't want to appear like an ungrateful brat, too spoiled to deal with reality.

"I understand my father has worries about my safety. It's just that—well, I've not had time to get used to all of this. Especially when I thought—"

"You thought what?"

She shrugged, while telling herself to step aside until there was three or four feet of distance separating them. That might be enough space to get her breathing back to an even keel. But looking into those dreamy eyes had done something to her feet. Both of them seemed stuck to the floor.

A nervous flutter suddenly attacked the back of her throat, forcing her to swallow before she could answer. "I thought—well, you see, like Nolan pointed out, this is my first real venture at living away from home. I was looking forward to it. Being just me—taking care of myself, doing things for myself. Now, all my plans have been turned upside down."

Before she could guess his intentions, he stepped forward and placed a hand on her shoulder. It felt big and warm, and the mere fact that he was touching her sent electrical currents shooting through her entire body.

"I promise, Savannah, this isn't going to be as bad as you're thinking. I will stay out of your way as much as possible. Okay?"

His voice was low, and husky, and just as seductive as the touch of his hand. "Okay," she murmured. "And I'll do my best not to cause you any major headaches."

One corner of his lips cocked upward. "Let's not worry about future problems. Certainly not for the rest of today."

His hand eased off her shoulder and Savannah decided it was high time to step away from him.

"I'm all for that." She walked over to the bags she'd dropped earlier and collected them from the floor. "Now if you'll excuse me, I'll take these to the bedroom."

Inside the master bedroom, Savannah placed her luggage on the end of a queen-sized bed with an ornate head- and footboard made of brass. A green and navy comforter, along with pillows in matching shams, covered the mattress. However, a quick peek beneath the comforter revealed there were no sheets. She made a mental note to put them on her shopping list.

The sound of Chaz's footsteps had her turning away from the bed to see him entering the room with her remaining bags.

"Where would you like these?" he asked.

"Anywhere will be fine. Thanks," she told him.

He put the suitcases on the floor at the foot of the bed, then promptly returned to the open doorway.

Pausing there, he asked, "Are you okay with this room?"

"The room is fine. But I realize I'm going to need more things than I anticipated. Does your bed have linen?"

"No. But I don't need a set of sheets to be able to sleep."

Not knowing how to respond to that, she simply said, "Oh."

Her one word reply put an amused look on his face. "I was in the army," he explained. "Fluffy beds with nice linens aren't always available to a soldier."

Intrigued, Savannah took a few steps toward him. "You were in the military?"

"For eight years."

She stared at him, while trying to picture him in a uniform, following the rigors of the army. "Eight years! Really?"

A faint smile touched his face. "I can see that surprises you."

"Very much. I thought—" She broke off as she realized that up until now, she'd not been thinking about Chaz's background. She'd been too preoccupied with the present and how to control her unsettling reaction to him.

"Thought what?" he prodded. "That I spent my younger years being a bouncer in some sleazy nightclub?"

Embarrassed heat swept over her face. "No! Not exactly. My father would never hire anyone without excellent credentials. I just assumed you had probably worked for a security firm or in law enforcement."

He shook his head. "After having army buddies around me for so many years, I wondered what it might be like to go solo. Turns out I like it."

He was talking about his work, but Savannah was thinking more along the lines of his love life. Did he also like living alone? That was definitely a question she was going to keep to herself. It was none of her business if Chaz shared an apartment with a woman, or dated a bevy of them.

"That's good. I mean—that you like working solo." Flustered by her straying thoughts and the way his lazy gaze continued to meander over her face, she purposely moved back to the bed and picked up one of the pillows. "There are so many things I need for the apartment. I'm going to put off unpacking and make a trip to the nearest shopping center."

"I'll have to go with you," he said. "So we'll take my car."

Frowning, she turned to look at him. "Are you planning on driving me everywhere I need to go? Because I've already booked a rental car. In fact, I'm supposed to pick it up this afternoon."

He stroked a thumb and forefinger over his black goatee as he contemplated her question. "We'll pick up the car after you finish your shopping. There might be occasions while you're at the university that I'll have to be elsewhere. But that doesn't mean I want you driving around town or to and from campus without me in the vehicle with you or following directly behind you."

She struggled to keep from rolling her eyes toward the ceiling. This had to be the most ridiculous waste she'd ever heard of, but she knew from experience it would be fruitless to argue the point with her father.

"Fine. At least, I'll have a car of my own," she said, then walked over to the door. "Now if you don't mind, I'd like to change clothes before we leave."

His dark gaze swept over her and Savannah got the feeling he'd already undressed her. The notion shot a plume of heat from her toes to her head.

"I'll be waiting in the living room."

He turned away and Savannah couldn't shut the door between them fast enough. After turning the lock, she slumped against the wooden panel and waited for her heart to quit pounding and her breaths to become more than shallow sups.

Dear Lord, what was the man doing to her? At this rate, she was going to end up fainting at his feet! A fate that would be worse than humiliating.

No, she thought, as she marched over to the bed and began to shed her blouse and skirt. Before she made a complete fool of herself, she was going to convince herself that she disliked everything about the sexy Latino. And that included his tall muscular body, those dark dreamy eyes and husky voice. She would trick her brain into believing she didn't find anything attractive in the way his black hair waved gently away from his face or the way his trimmed mustache bracketed a pair of very kissable lips.

Kissable?

Damn! What did she know about kissing a man? Not just a young college boy, but a mature, masculine hunk of man like Chaz Mendoza? Very little. And while she was here in Austin, she didn't plan on learning.

She was here to study diseases. Not to fall prey to a chronic heart condition.

Chapter Three

"I hate to tell you this, Savannah, but I'm not sure we're going to get everything loaded into the car," Chaz told her, as he positioned sacks of groceries into the back seat.

For the past few hours, he'd followed her around an up-scale department store while she gathered bed and bathroom linens, along with dishes, cookware and kitchen utensils. Those items were jammed tightly in the trunk. Since then, they'd moved on to a nearby supermarket where she'd filled three baskets with anything and everything that happened to catch her fancy.

"No problem," she told him. "I'll go back inside and tell customer service we need to have the rest of our purchases delivered to the apartment."

Something about her words and the way she'd said them reminded him of Allison. And suddenly he was thinking back to a time when his heart had been open and the future had been as bright as a blue sky. But that had all slowly and surely changed.

Shaking away the memories, he said, "Wait a minute before you do that. I might be able to fit everything in."

He emerged from the back seat and as he looked at her standing there so chic and pretty in a pair of tight black jeans and a white off-the-shoulder blouse, he was reminded that she was a Fortune. Money made it easy to fix most of their problems. On the other hand, it sometimes created huge difficulties for them and for the people who tried to love them.

"You're thinking I've gone overboard." Tilting her head from side to side, she contemplated the remaining sacks to be loaded into the car. "Maybe I did get a little carried away. But I like to eat. Don't you?"

"It is an enjoyable necessity," he answered. "From the looks of all this, I think you have enough food to last for weeks."

"Not the fresh things like milk and vegetables. Our cook at home told me those sorts of things only last a week or so."

Chaz doubted she'd ever prepared anything more than a peanut-butter-and-jelly sandwich and that simple task would probably be stretching the limit of her cooking skills. But she seemed eager and excited about trying her hand in the kitchen and Chaz had no desire to burst her bubble.

To be honest, he already felt bad enough about Savannah's plans being thwarted by her father. Chaz was thirty-one, but he still remembered how excited he'd felt when he'd first ventured out on his own, away from the watchful eye of his father, Esteban, and older brothers, Carlo and Mark. He'd been like a young stallion finally released from the corral. If his father had hired a bodyguard to follow him, Chaz would've put up a far bigger fuss than Savannah had.

Pulling his thoughts back to the present moment, he

said, "With all that cold cereal you bought, I'm sure the milk will be used before it spoils."

She chuckled. "I guess you noticed I like the round fruity cereal that's coated with sugar. Awful of me, isn't it? I study diseases and I've learned how bad sugar is for me. But I confess. I have a sweet tooth. That's probably my worst sin. That and losing my temper."

She considered eating sugared cereal and getting angry her worst sins? At the age of twenty-five, could she really be that innocent? Miles had described his daughter as always studying instead of enjoying any kind of nightlife. Maybe the man had been right about that part of Savannah's life. Still, she was so beautiful and sexy that it was hard for Chaz to imagine there hadn't been a line of young men knocking on her door, begging for dates.

Unable to keep a grin off his face, he said, "Well, we all have our vices," he said with a grin. "And yours don't sound that bad to me."

Five minutes later, the car was loaded without any extra space to spare. From the supermarket, Chaz drove them straight to the car rental company where Savannah's vehicle was waiting for her.

Apparently, special perks came with having the last name of Fortune. Savannah didn't have to wait. As soon as she presented her ID, she signed a paper and was handed the key to a small cream-colored luxury car.

"I'm assuming you have your license and you know how to drive," Chaz commented, as she slid into the driver's seat.

Smiling impishly up at him, she snapped the seat belt in place. "I do. I have a car of my own at home, but Dad didn't want me driving alone all the way from New Orleans to Austin. I'll tell you a secret, though. Back in New Orleans, I do ride the streetcar at times."

"Why is that a secret?"

She laughed and the sound was as happy as the expression on her face. It made him want to laugh with her.

"Because Dad doesn't want any of his children to use public transportation. It's too dangerous, or so he says. See, even before this thing with Charlotte Robinson became a problem, Dad was always worried about kidnappers. But I never make riding the streetcar a routine habit."

The image of some evil man snatching Savannah and holding her for ransom was enough to make Chaz vow to never take his eyes off her.

"All I can say is thank God you're not in New Orleans now."

"What does that mean?"

"Nothing." He shut the car door and leaned his head partially into the open window. "Since you don't know your way around Austin yet, you'd better follow me. Be sure and stay close to my car. And keep your cell phone handy just in case a traffic light or merging vehicles separate us and you get lost."

"I have a navigational system on the dashboard and also on my cell phone. I'm not going to get lost," she assured him. "But I have my phone and your number—if I need you."

If I need you. Obviously, Savannah didn't feel a bit threatened at the thought of a crazy woman out to harm her or her family. And she certainly didn't think she would ever need Chaz for any reason.

Somehow, that didn't surprise him. But the fact that it bothered him did.

To Chaz's relief, the drive back to Live Oak Lane went without incident. When they reached her apartment, he allowed Savannah to park her vehicle beneath the protective cover of the carport. He parked directly behind her and opened the trunk to begin the task of transporting her purchases into the building.

She was all smiles and energy as she joined him at the back of his car. "Now comes the fun part," she said. "I can't wait to get all this stuff into place. It should make the apartment feel more like home."

Home. Chaz didn't think of that word very often. The connotation wasn't the same for him as it was for most people. Maybe that was because he'd spent eight years in the army, where home had meant a bed in a barrack or a sleeping bag beneath a tent. Or perhaps it was because as a boy growing up, his home hadn't always been a warm, loving environment with two happy parents.

"I'm sure you'll make it comfortable," he replied, then lifted out one of the bigger boxes, containing a set of cookware. "I'll get the heavy things. Can you handle some of the lighter grocery bags?"

"Of course I can. I'm not weak or helpless."

No. She was rich, and beautiful, and accustomed to having everything done for her, Chaz thought. Still, he had to give her credit. Today, she seemed very eager to do chores for herself.

"Okay. Let's get to work."

Two hours later, Savannah was still arranging things in the apartment when Chaz retreated to the back patio to take a quiet break and enjoy the last of the waning twilight. Yet, no sooner had he taken a seat on the red glider than his cell phone rang.

Groaning, he checked the caller ID, then seeing it was his older brother, he promptly punched the accept button.

"Hey, Carlo," he greeted. "What's up?"

"Not much. Schuyler and I are here at La Viña about to have dinner."

"Anything wrong? The security systems all on go?"

Since Chaz had moved to Austin to join his family and the expanding Mendoza businesses, he'd taken on the responsibility of the security for both the winery and the restaurant. So far, he'd installed a sophisticated security system that enabled him to control and monitor everything from his laptop or phone. He'd also hired dependable, experienced guards to keep a human eye on both properties. The expense had been more than his family had wanted to invest in the businesses, but Chaz had argued that a break-in or a tipsy, sue-happy customer would be far more costly.

Carlo quickly reassured him. "Relax. Everything is fine. No problems. I hadn't seen you around today and Dad explained that you'd started a new undertaking."

At the moment, Chaz felt as though he'd taken on about ten jobs rather than one. And the night hadn't yet started. He could only imagine what Savannah was going to ask him to do next.

"That's right. I'm watching over Savannah Fortune. She's from New Orleans. And a cousin to Schuyler, by the way."

"So I've heard. And my wife also informs me that Savannah Fortune is twenty-five and very pretty. Along with highly intelligent. How did you manage to get this gig, little brother? Does Miles Fortune know you're a danger around women?"

Chaz chuckled. They both knew that Carlo had been far more of a ladies' man than Chaz had ever thought to be. But his brother had experienced a complete change once he'd fallen in love and married Schuyler Fortunado. Chaz would be the first one to admit he'd had his doubts about his brother getting married and settling down, but Carlo had proven him wrong. So far, he seemed blissfully happy in the role of a doting husband.

Chaz said, "No worries there. Savannah is far from my type. Besides, I'm here to protect her. Not seduce her."

Chaz could hear soft music and a faint murmur of diners talking in the background. The mental image of the restaurant had him longing for a plate of ravioli or eggplant parmesan and a glass of Mendoza wine.

Nolan had suggested that Chaz take Savannah for an evening meal, but that wasn't going to happen. No. While working as a bodyguard, Chaz never mixed business with pleasure. And he didn't plan on starting now.

"Not your type, huh? I seem to remember a time when rich and pretty was your type. For several years, in fact."

Chaz tried not to wince at his brother's remark. It was rare that any of his family brought up his broken relationship with Allison. After so many years, Chaz had tried to forget and he wished the rest of his family would keep the past in the past.

"Allison was a long time ago, Carlo. And I learned that her type wasn't my type at all."

"Damn, Chaz, what's eating you?"

Chaz closed his eyes and rubbed a hand against his forehead. "Who said anything was eating at me?"

"The tone of your voice. You sound like you could bend a crowbar with your bare hands."

He bit back a sigh. "Sorry. Today has been—let's just say it's been nothing like I expected."

"Look, Chaz, I obviously don't know what's going on with you and Miss Fortune. But if you feel uncomfortable about this job, then you should let Miles Fortune know you want out. Better now than later."

Chaz hated to admit it, but he did want out. Ever since

he'd spotted Savannah at the airport, he'd had bad vibes about the whole situation. This wasn't his usual bodyguard stint where he accompanied a wealthy man on a risky overseas business trip. Or provided security for a banker during his commute to and from work. This was going to be an up close and personal job. He was going to be living with Savannah on a 24/7 schedule. And he wasn't sure he was capable of resisting that much temptation.

"I'm not a quitter, Carlo. I started this job and I fully intend to see it to the finish."

"Somehow that doesn't surprise me," Carlo told him, then added thoughtfully, "Frankly, I'm wondering who put Miles Fortune on to you for this job."

"I didn't ask the man," Chaz admitted. "I'm assuming it was Connor Fortunado. He's the one who discovered Charlotte Robinson has been digging around for information about Miles's family."

"Well, with Miles being a half brother to Gerald, there's definitely a strong connection between the two families. Even if they've not associated with each other through the years. I'm telling you, Chaz, the thought of Charlotte out there plotting against the Fortunes—any Fortune—has me worried about Schuyler's safety. I find myself not wanting to let her out of my sight. And though looking at my beautiful wife is a treat, I can't follow her around all day and take care of my other duties."

Chaz said, "I take it she's not sitting there at the table with you now."

"No. She's gone to the powder room. Matter of fact, she's been gone for several minutes now. If she doesn't return to our table soon, I'm going to have to go searching for her."

"Calm down. She probably ran into a friend and got to chatting. As for the uncertainties over Charlotte, I wouldn't worry, Carlo. Schuyler is a smart woman. She isn't going to take unnecessary chances. She understands the danger Charlotte poses." *Unlike Savannah*, Chaz thought. She considered the problem to be about as serious as a pesky fly at a picnic table.

Carlo suddenly said, "Ah, I see my wife coming this way. Thank God. I'd better get off the phone, Chaz. Will you be coming by the winery tomorrow?"

"I'm planning on it. Unless some unforeseen problem pops up."

"Okay. See you later, brother."

Carlo broke the connection and Chaz was slipping the phone back into the pocket on his shirt when the back door to the apartment opened and Savannah stepped onto the patio.

For the third time today, she'd changed clothes. This time she'd exchanged the jeans and blouse for a pair of gray jersey gym shorts and a cropped T-shirt of the same fabric. As she walked toward him, Chaz tried not to notice the perfect shape of her legs or how the golden tan of her skin reminded him of creamy caramel.

She glanced around the small yard enclosed with a wooden privacy fence before taking a seat in the chair opposite him. "This is nice out here. The evening air has actually turned cool."

"Yes. It's pleasant," he agreed.

She reached up and adjusted the rubber band holding her brown ponytail to the back of her head. The upward movement of her arms caused Chaz's gaze to slip to the gentle thrust of her breasts. Even though she was small all over, she was perfectly proportioned and Chaz found himself imagining how she would look wearing nothing at all. He figured her breasts would be firm and perky with little brownish-pink nipples that would fit, oh, so sweetly between his lips.

The sound of her voice suddenly jerked at his straying thoughts and he hoped the darkening shadows hid the hot color he felt creeping up his neck.

"Do you like being outdoors?" she asked. "I mean, doing sports and things? Some of my brothers enjoy sports like soccer and fishing out in the gulf."

"I've played sports before. Mostly baseball. But I've not done any of that in a long time. Work and…other things get in the way. What about you? Do you like the outdoors?"

Her nose wrinkled in an impish fashion. "When I was a girl I loved it. I liked helping the gardener tend the flowers. Mother has always insisted on having beautiful flowers in the yard and I especially loved taking care of the camellias. But as you said, college and other things eventually took over my time."

Chaz found it hard to imagine Savannah's pretty little hands digging into the earth or using a pair of pruning shears. When he'd shaken her hand at the airport, he'd noticed her skin had been as smooth as a satin sheet. And though her fingernails were a short, practical length, they were beautifully manicured and painted a pale coral color.

He didn't make a reply, mostly because he knew it wasn't a good idea to engage in personal conversation with a client. But his lack of conversation hardly seemed to put her off. And a part of him was pleased that she wanted to interact with him.

She asked, "Do you ever snow ski?"

"I know how to ski, if that's what you mean. Do you?"

"Oh, sure. It's probably the only sport I've learned to do well enough to enjoy. Every winter, my sisters and I try to go to Arapahoe Basin or Telluride."

"And your father allows you and your sisters to travel out to Colorado alone?"

She grimaced. "No. We always have to persuade one brother, at least, into going with us. I imagine with all this worry over Charlotte Robinson, Dad is going to try and curtail all his children's travels."

"Probably. But sooner or later this thing with her will eventually come to an end," he suggested. "And your lives will return to normal."

"I can only hope you're right." She wrinkled her nose again and then smiled at him. "Do you know what I'd really like to do in Colorado?"

Actually, Chaz found it much easier to imagine Savannah on an exotic sandy island wearing a string bikini than in a mountain village bundled against the cold.

"Other than ski?" he asked. "I couldn't guess."

"Don't laugh. But I'd like to hike the San Juan Mountains. They're full of old mines dug by prospectors during the silver and gold rush days. I'd love to see how those adventurous men, and few hearty women, must have lived in those days."

She couldn't have said anything to surprise him more. "That's history. I thought you were a science person."

"Oh, I'm definitely a science person. My main objective in life is to get my doctorate and hopefully someday help in controlling or completely wiping out a disease. But most every person likes to dream about something adventurous and fun. Exploring the mountains is a dream of mine." She shrugged. "I doubt it will ever come true. But that's okay. I'll still have my dream."

This was not the person he had been expecting Savannah Fortune to be. All through the day, he'd been waiting for her to break into tears, to admit that she was too overwhelmed with the chore of setting up the apartment to make it livable. He'd thought that once she got into the kitchen, she'd wring her hands together and start an immediate search for a cook/housekeeper. Instead, she'd managed to brew a pitcher of iced tea and make a plate of cold-cut sandwiches. And in spite of Chaz insisting that he would take care of his own meals and didn't expect her to supply them, she'd made an issue of him joining her for the little lunch.

"You surprise me, Savannah. Most young women like you wouldn't be interested in that sort of thing."

Her eyes narrowed slightly. "Women like me? What does that mean?"

How could three little words make a man feel like he was suddenly trying to balance himself on a high wire? In an effort to ease the tension, he crossed his ankles out in front of him.

"Nothing insulting if that's what you're thinking. I only meant that you're young and wealthy enough to visit any spot in the world. And just looking at you, I'd think you'd be interested in seeing Paris or London, or even Monte Carlo. Not hiking around the San Juans to look at old mines."

She smiled and Chaz was relieved that he must have said something right.

"I'm getting the idea that you don't know much about women, Chaz. But you're soon going to learn that I'm not one-dimensional or typical. And being petite and feminine doesn't make me a softie."

No, she definitely wasn't typical. But she certainly looked like a softie to him. Soft from the top of her dark brown head all the way to her pink painted toenails.

Smiling faintly, he said, "Well, you might not believe this, but I like your dream."

The pleased look on her face was so charming Chaz found it impossible to tear his gaze away.

"Really? Then maybe we could make the trip together sometime. You could go as my bodyguard. That should make Dad happy. But I'd really just want you to go as a friend."

Chaz seriously doubted Miles Fortune would want him near Savannah in any other capacity than as a bodyguard. And to be honest with himself, Chaz didn't think he could ever be just a friend to Savannah. So that meant the only choice he had was to keep his distance from the woman. Emotionally and physically.

"That's nice of you, Savannah," he said, making his voice purposely stilted. "Perhaps we could do that. Someday."

Her eyes widened just a fraction and then she rubbed her palms up and down her thighs in an awkward gesture. Chaz could see his curt tone had hurt her and he hated himself for using it. But he had to keep her at arm's length. Even if it meant making her dislike him.

Rising from the chair, she said, "I—uh, need to be getting back inside." She turned toward the apartment, then made a swift about-face. "I almost forgot. I came out here to ask you about your bed."

He stared at her as his mind leaped in all sorts of crazy directions. "My bed?"

"Yes. To see if you knew how to put on the sheets. Or would you like for me to do it?"

She was offering to do the chore for him. He didn't know whether he wanted to laugh or groan. But he did know one damned thing. And that was how much he wanted to take Miss Savannah Fortune into his arms and kiss those cherry-ripe lips until her arms were wrapped tightly around his neck and he forgot that he was only her protector.

"Look, Savannah, you don't need to do anything for me. I can manage my own chores. And that includes making up my own bed."

Her lips flattened to a thin line. "Oh. My mistake. With you being a bachelor, I gather you've learned how to do household things for yourself. I'm not sure if any of my brothers have ever made up a bed. But you're—uh—not like them."

No. He'd not been raised in a privileged family. His parents' marriage had been passionate enough to produce five sons. But eventually the spark between Esteban and Ginger had been extinguished by his love of wine and women. Ginger had tolerated her husband's philandering for as long as she could before she'd finally sought a divorce and walked away. Yet, in spite of Esteban's faults, he'd basically been a good father and made sure his five sons remained together and grew into responsible adults. Even so, Chaz's younger years hadn't been easy.

But Savannah didn't need to know about his personal life, Chaz decided. And frankly, he didn't need to know about hers. Yet, he couldn't deny that he wanted to learn every single detail about her past and the present. He wanted to know what drove her to be the woman she was and hoped to be someday.

"Listen, Savannah, if you don't know how to make a bed before you enter the army, you'll learn soon after. And learn to do it perfectly. Otherwise, a soldier would find himself in trouble at inspection time."

"I see. Then you don't need my help at all."

She turned and walked back into the apartment and as Chaz watched her go, he wondered why he wasn't feeling relieved. And why everything inside him wanted to call her back.

Chapter Four

Early the next morning, Savannah sat at the kitchen table in a pair of blue silk pajamas and a robe. With both hands clutching one of the red cups she'd purchased yesterday, she took a long, grateful sip of steaming coffee.

After the extensive day of traveling, shopping and setting up the apartment, Savannah had expected to fall asleep the moment her head hit the pillow. Instead, she'd tossed and turned, while blaming her insomnia on the extra-firm mattress and unfamiliar surroundings. But deep down, she recognized it was neither of those things that had made her lose sleep last night. It had been Chaz Mendoza and her unexplainable reaction to him.

Damn the man. Why did he have to be such a perfect masculine specimen? What was it about his rugged features that made her want to sigh, that made her dream of touching him, kissing him?

Thank goodness tomorrow was Monday, she thought, as she attempted to push away the ridiculous questions roaming around in her head. She'd be starting her research studies at the university in the morning. She'd finally be able to get away from Chaz and get her mind on something important. Instead of daydreaming like a silly high school girl mooning after the star athlete.

The smartphone lying near her left arm chirped to signal a new text message had arrived. The sound interrupted Savannah's troubled thoughts and she glanced down to see a short message from her father illuminated on the screen.

Are you getting settled? Is Mr. Mendoza taking care of you?

Taking care of her? Chaz had upended everything! She wanted to yell out the response in loud capital letters. Instead, she drew in a deep, calming breath and began to tap out a quick reassuring note to her father. The last thing she wanted was for Miles to start ringing the phone, demanding an explanation to ambiguous words. Their relationship was already strained. If she lost her temper while talking with him, it would only make matters worse. She could already see him standing at the front door with intentions of carting her back to New Orleans.

Moments later, she was punching the send button when she heard footsteps. Glancing over her shoulder, she saw Chaz, fully dressed in khakis and a white polo shirt, entering the kitchen. Unlike her, he looked alert and fully refreshed. No doubt, he'd had a nice restful sleep, while she'd been staring at the shadows on the ceiling, wondering how she was going to ignore the man for the next few weeks. It was going to be an impossible task.

"Good morning," she greeted. "The coffee is only a few minutes old so it should still be good. Help yourself."

"Thanks. I will."

You don't need to do anything for me. I can manage my own chores.

The memory of his stiff remarks last night still stung. And she continued to ask herself why she hadn't flung some flippant retort back at him. If he'd been any other man on earth, she would've told him to go jump off a cliff or into the deepest lake he could find. Instead, she'd walked away and wondered what had caused the abrupt change in him. One minute he'd seemed warm and approachable, then the next minute he'd turned cool and distant.

He carried a cup of black coffee over to the round wooden table and sat down on the opposite side from her.

Savannah felt her pulse leap into a faster pace and knew the reaction had nothing to do with the small amount of caffeine she'd consumed.

"How was your night?" he asked, his gaze glued to the brown liquid in his cup.

"Great. I woke up before the alarm went off."

His gaze lifted to her face and Savannah felt another jolt to her senses.

"You need an alarm on Sunday morning?" he asked. "You must be going to church."

"I do usually go to early mass. But not today. I need to find a church first. Preferably, one that's close by. As for the alarm, I always set it. Sleeping in makes me feel sluggish for the remainder of the day."

"I see," he said, then asked, "So you will be planning on church next Sunday?"

"Yes. Definitely. Why? Surely you don't think a trip to church is risky."

"Doesn't matter. I'll be with you one way or the other."

The moment Savannah felt her mouth start to fall open

she promptly clamped it tight. Yesterday, after she'd gotten over the shock and anger of her father hiring a bodyguard, she'd decided going against Chaz would only make things worse. She wanted to show him that she harbored no ill will toward him. In fact, she liked him. But last evening on the patio, he'd made it clear that he didn't want to be her friend. Therefore, she had to respect his wishes and keep her distance from him in every way.

"Fine," she said. "I'll let you know my plans long before next Sunday."

She went over to the cabinets and began to gather a bowl and a spoon for cereal. By the time she returned to the table with her breakfast, she felt bad about not offering him something to eat. But he knew where she'd stored everything and like he'd so succinctly told her, he didn't need her to take care of him.

She'd taken several bites of the sweetened oats when she noticed he was watching her. Awkwardly, she balanced her spoon on the side of the bowl and looked directly at him.

"Do I have milk on my face or something?"

His gaze slowly and deliberately slipped over her. "No. I was about to ask you what you were planning to do today."

She shrugged. "I need to organize the notes and books I'll be taking to the university tomorrow. Other than that, I don't have anything planned. So don't worry. You won't have to follow me around the supermarket again."

He curled both hands around the coffee mug and Savannah found herself staring at the long fingers, imagining how it might feel to have them curled around her breasts.

Oh, my. Where were these wild thoughts coming

from? And how loud would he laugh if he could read her mind?

He said, "You don't have to be so snippy about it."

His comment took her by surprise. "Snippy? I'm merely being the way you want me to be."

She saw a look of confusion in his brown eyes and then a light of dawning pushed the blank fog away. "Savannah, you're wrong. I don't want any such thing."

"Oh, yes. You do. That makes it easier for you to dislike me."

He sat straight up in his chair and stared at her. Savannah deliberately went back to eating her cereal. But inside, her heart was pounding and her lungs felt as though they'd forgotten how to pull in air or push it out.

"Okay. So I'm off base," she said. "I'll tell you the same way you told me yesterday. It doesn't matter whether you like me or not. It's your job to protect me. And that's the only reason you're sitting here at my kitchen table."

He frowned. "Ouch. Something must have stung you last night. Did you check your bed for bedbugs?"

Something had stung her all right, Savannah thought. But she'd be damned before she let it happen again. "The bed is exceptionally clean."

He went back to drinking his coffee and she forced herself to focus on the bowl of cereal.

After a stretch of awkward silence, he said, "I told my brother I'd show up at the winery today."

"Okay."

When he didn't say more, she glanced across the table to see a thoughtful frown on his face.

"Is that all?" she asked. "Or were you about to tell me that while you're gone I need to remain inside the apartment and bolt all the doors?"

"I was going to say something like that. But I've changed my mind."

Savannah suspected that was something that didn't happen often with Chaz. He seemed like a man who knew the direction he wanted to take and nothing would change his mind to steer him off course.

"Oh. Then you're going to tell me to get the keys to the Lincoln and have fun driving to wherever I want to go."

A wry smile slanted his lips. "No. That isn't going to happen. Not while I'm responsible for your safety."

And how long was that actually going to be? Savannah had been thinking he'd be around for the duration of her studies. But perhaps she'd been wrong. After a few days, he might decide he wanted no more of her, or the job.

Strange how yesterday that thought would have made her a happy woman. Yet, today the idea of him leaving was a bit deflating. Oh, Lord, she was clearly getting messed up in the head.

"I understand you have responsibilities other than me," she replied. "But I'm not going to lock myself in the closet while you deal with them."

His brows lifted. "The closets in this apartment have locks on them? I hadn't noticed."

Rolling her eyes, she picked up her partially eaten breakfast and carried it over to the sink. "You'd better keep your bodyguard job. I don't think you'd make it as a stand-up comedian."

He walked over to where Savannah was pouring the remains of her cereal down the garbage disposal. As he stood next to her, she caught the faint scent of earthy cologne and felt the warmth of his body radiating toward hers.

"I never was too good at telling jokes," he said. "Or making conversation. Not like my brothers."

Was that his way of explaining his warm-one-minute-and-cool-the-next attitude? In spite of her resolution to keep a reserved distance between them, she couldn't stop herself from asking, "You have more than one brother?"

"I have four brothers. No sisters."

She turned her gaze in his direction and suddenly she was taking in his rich brown eyes, tanned skin, and the black mustache and goatee framing his lips. How many women had skimmed their fingertips along his jaw, she wondered. How many had experienced the taste of his lips?

It doesn't matter. It can't matter.

Swallowing hard, she placed the bowl in the sink and filled it with water. "Are your brothers anything like you?"

"I wouldn't say so. We might resemble each other in some ways. But we're all different. I'm sure it's that way with you and your siblings."

"That's true. We all have different looks and personalities."

Feeling certain that she was going to collapse from a lack of oxygen if she didn't move away from him, Savannah walked back over to the table.

To her surprise, he followed her.

"Uh—back to the winery," he said. "I was thinking you might want to join me."

She tried to hide her surprise. "Go with you? Why? So you won't have to worry about leaving me here alone?"

He grimaced. "Damn it, Savannah. Do you have to make everything difficult? Yes. That is one of the reasons for the invitation. I'm not going to leave you here alone. But I also thought you might like to see the place. Mendoza Winery is becoming rather popular with folks in the area. And making wine is sort of a science—that's your field."

"Yes, it's my field. But making wine is a long way from finding a cure for a disease."

He suddenly grinned. "Who knows? Someday you might learn there's a lifesaving effect in fermented grapes."

She'd never expected anything like this from the man. He almost made it sound like he wanted her company. And the dimples that were coming and going at the corners of his lips were impossible to resist.

"Hmm. I can't argue that point." She smiled at him. "Okay, I'd like to join you. When were you planning on going?"

"In a couple of hours."

"I'll be ready," she told him.

Chaz didn't do things on impulse and he'd thought long and hard about inviting Savannah to join him on the trip to the winery before he actually asked her. Any way he looked at the situation, he'd recognized his options weren't good. No way would he leave her here in the apartment, alone and unprotected. On the other hand, taking her with him to the winery made it appear as though the trip were a personal outing. Which might give her the wrong idea. Not only her, but what was his father and brother going to think when he showed up with Savannah?

The question had him glancing over to where she sat in the passenger seat of his car, gazing curiously out the side window.

She looked adorably feminine in a pale pink sundress that fit her bodice snuggly and fluttered around her shapely calves. Tiny straps were tied in bows at the top of each bare shoulder and each time Chaz looked at her, the idea of untying those bows flitted through his mind.

He must have sighed because she suddenly turned her head and looked at him.

"Are you okay?"

No, he was in the worst mess he could ever remember getting himself into, Chaz thought. And there was no way to jump out of it. Unless he didn't care about looking like a cowardly quitter. No, he thought ruefully, he had to power forward and make the best of the situation.

"Sure. Just concentrating on the traffic," he lied. "It's rather busy for Sunday morning."

"Since I've only been to Austin once before, I really couldn't say about the traffic," she said.

"I'm assuming that one time was when part of the Robinson estate burned."

"That's right. My siblings and I had come up here to attend Schuyler's family reunion and meet some of our Fortune relatives. But none of Gerald's children showed up and we were all thinking they weren't interested in meeting our line of the family. Then Olivia came running in with the news that a fire had occurred and Ben had been seriously injured."

"That had to be an inauspicious meeting with your cousins."

"It was under strained conditions," she agreed. "Naturally, everyone was worried about Ben. And everyone was speculating about the fire and how it might have started."

"Have you contacted any of your cousins since then?"

She shook her head. "The only one I've talked with is your sister-in-law, Schuyler. She called to express her regret on how everything turned out."

"Hmm. She had high hopes for that reunion. And I

think when this problem with Charlotte is over, she'll probably try again at getting the Fortune families together. See, Schuyler is a positive, happy person and she believes everyone should feel as she does."

His gaze left the traffic long enough to see Savannah's lips tilt into a faint smile.

She said, "I liked her as soon as I met her. You're very fortunate to have her for a sister-in-law."

"She makes my brother Carlo very happy. That makes me glad she's come into the Mendoza family."

"I feel the same way about Lizzie. The joy she's given Nolan makes me love her even more. And their baby daughter is so precious. While I'm here in Austin, I'm hoping I'll get to be more of an aunt to little Stella."

Before Savannah had arrived in Austin, Chaz would've never expected her to be gushing over a baby. Sure, she was female, but Miles had described his daughter as having little to no interest in anything outside of her science studies. *Miles Fortune must be too busy making money to see the real Savannah*, Chaz thought. So far, he'd found her to be multifaceted with all the desires of a normal woman.

"At the time your father hired me, he gave me a brief rundown of your family," Chaz told her. "If I remember correctly, Nolan is the only one of you who's married."

"Yes, as of now he's the only one married," she replied. "What about your brothers? Is Carlo the lone family man?"

He hesitated, but only for a brief moment. "No. I have a half brother, Joaquin, who's married also. Actually, to another one of your Fortune cousins, Zoe."

"Zoe?" A thoughtful frown creased her brow before a look of dawning came over her. "Are you talking about Gerald Robinson's daughter Zoe?"

"That's her."

"Yes. I did meet her briefly at the Robinson estate. It was shortly after the fire and everything was chaotic. But I recall a tall dark man being with her. She probably introduced him as her husband, but there were so many names and faces that night it's hard to keep them all straight in my memory."

"I'm sure that would've been Joaquin. He's a business consultant and she works in her father's tech business. That's how the two of them met."

She turned in the seat so that she was facing him. "Well, this is intriguing. You have two brothers who are married to Fortune women. I had no idea that you were that connected to my family. It's no wonder Dad hired you."

Actually, Chaz had four cousins and an uncle who had also married into different branches of the Fortunes, and a few more cousins living in Red Rock who'd also married into the Fortune family, but now wasn't the time to go into all those family ties. He didn't want Savannah getting the idea that every time a Mendoza got close to a Fortune wedding bells were destined to ring. Which, in his case, couldn't be further from the truth. He wasn't like his successful brothers. Allison had taught him that much when she'd moved on to a life without him.

Trying not to let those bitter memories tarnish the bright Sunday morning, he said, "I have no idea if that had any impact on Mr. Fortune's decision to hire me. But with us having mutual relatives—by marriage, that is—it does help me understand the situation much better."

"Situation?"

"With Gerald's ex-wife," he explained.

"Hmm. Yes, I can see where it would give you a better insight to the family connections," she said after a thoughtful moment. "It surprises me, though, that the two of your brothers who are married chose to hook up with a Fortune woman."

At least she wasn't asking him how he happened to have a half brother, Chaz thought. He wasn't ready to explain how his father had had an affair with his brother, Orlando's, girlfriend. The illicit union had produced a son and ultimately caused years of bitter estrangement between Chaz's father and his uncle. Thank God, the two men had gotten past all the wrongdoing and forgiven each other. Still, it would be awkward to admit to Savannah that his father had once been an adulterer.

"There are some very beautiful women in the Fortune family," he reasoned. "And the Mendoza men are known for being attracted to beautiful women."

From the corner of his eye, he could see her brows arch with speculation.

"Does that include you?"

"I'm not totally immune to them," he answered, then feeling a great need to change the subject, he pointed to a dingy brown building wedged between a warehouse and a barbershop. "If you like country music, that's the place to go. Some of the best unknowns sing and play there."

She peered out the windshield at the row of buildings on the left side of the street. "Really? The building looks a bit ratty to me."

"That's one of the reasons it's the best night spot to visit. It isn't jammed with tourists."

"I like country music but the blues is my first choice. In New Orleans, we have some of the best blues musicians and down in the French Quarter you can listen to them most any time of the day or night."

"Do you live anywhere near the French Quarter?" he asked curiously.

"No. I still live with my parents—in the Garden District. That's where—"

"All the mansions and genteel people live," he finished for her.

Braking the car to a halt at a red light, he glanced over to see that a pretty pink color had washed over her cheeks.

She said, "You make it sound boring."

"On the contrary. I don't think anywhere in the city of New Orleans would be boring," he told her. *Especially with you for company*, he silently added.

"Well, to be honest, I've wanted a house of my own in the French Quarter. And someday I plan to buy one."

"Someday? Why not now?"

She shook her head. "At this point in my life, my studies come before everything. But later, when I'm finished with my degree and I'm financially independent from my family, I'll go house hunting."

Chaz could easily picture her in one of those three-story homes with a balcony made of scrolled ironwork overlooking the street. No doubt, she'd choose one with a private courtyard filled with tropical plants and hot, humid air that begged a person to sit and sip a cold mint julep. She had that southern mystique about her and New Orleans was where she belonged. Yet, Chaz was already wondering how he was going to feel once this job was over, and Savannah went back home to Louisiana.

Chapter Five

With the outskirts of the city disappearing behind them, Chaz guided the car off the main highway and onto a narrow farm-to-market road. The countryside swiftly turned to sloping hills and suddenly Savannah was gazing with amazement at acres and acres of carefully cultivated grapevines. Bright spring sunshine glinted off the dew-drenched leaves, while small bluebirds darted among the twisted vines. Here and there, large clusters of green grapes emerged from the leaves to bask in the warm sun.

"This is so lovely, Chaz! That night when my siblings and I drove out here for Schuyler's reunion, it was already dark, so I missed seeing the vineyard. Does this land belong to your family, as well as the winery?"

"It does," he replied. "Along with the vineyards, the winery and the restaurant, we also have a distribution center located in Austin Commons. We store much of our product there. And the family is currently working on plans to open a retail shop, a wine bar and a nightclub on a popular downtown street. In fact, Carlo and Schuyler have already purchased a nice piece of property for the nightclub."

"Wow, sounds like the Mendozas are not only hard working—they're also an ambitious bunch."

"When my family first started the winery, I'm not sure that anyone believed it would be as successful as it's turned out to be. Then as the wine began to catch on with the public, the business took off in all directions and one thing led to another. That's one of the reasons I moved here to Austin."

"You had a chance to become a part owner?"

His lips took on a wry twist. "No. But we've always been a close bunch and I wanted to be around to help with the family business."

Not only had he invited her on this trip, Savannah thought, but now he was talking about his personal life. Well, not exactly the private side of it, but he was talking about his family and she considered that to be personal. She didn't know what had brought about the change in him from last night to this morning, but she definitely liked it.

"And how is that working out?" she ventured to ask. "Are you glad you made the move?"

"I thought long and hard before leaving the army," he admitted. "After eight years, the military had pretty much become my whole life. And I had plans to become an MP. But then I started getting word from my dad and brothers about how the business here in Austin was doing handsprings and they needed my help with security. The thought of being with my family won out. Now it feels good to be contributing to the cause and being paid a nice salary, too."

"Mmm. That must be nice. To feel needed. By the time I reached middle school, I could see that Dad would never need me to contribute to Fortune Investments. He'd already made millions of dollars and had his own group of people to help run things. As I grew older, he never encouraged me to become a part of it. Frankly, it's probably for the best that he didn't. I'm not a business-minded person. I wouldn't be happy dealing with money and investments and things of that nature."

"I'm not a business-minded person, either," he admitted. "That's why I do security. It's what I'm trained for." He gestured up ahead. "Here we are."

Savannah looked away from him and out the windshield to see a huge building partially hidden beyond a group of shade trees. A perfectly landscaped lawn sloped all the way down to the road.

"Oh! Everything looks so different in the daylight. This is beautiful!"

She glanced over to see he was scanning the grounds with a keen gaze, as though he were assessing every detail for the slightest hint of a change, or a problem. The security of the winery was his job. Yet, he now had her safety to consider, too. Clearly, his responsibilities were far more than standing around looking strong and intimidating. Yesterday, she'd not fully understood that. Today, she was beginning to see everything from a different perspective.

"My brother's car is here, along with Dad's," he said. "Otherwise, it looks as though the place is quiet right now."

He parked the car in a graveled area shaded by a huge live oak, then skirted around to the passenger door to help her to the ground. The moment his strong hand came around hers, Savannah felt a surge of pleasure that had her wishing he'd continue to hold on to her. But the moment she was steady on her feet, he released her hand and she had to be satisfied with simply walking along by his side.

"I am properly impressed," she told him as she surveyed their surroundings. "Everything looks perfectly groomed."

He smiled at her and Savannah felt her breath catch in her throat. Looking at Chaz from any angle was a pleasure, she decided, but when he smiled, he was sinfully gorgeous. And far too much for her senses to handle.

"I'm glad you approve. It's all been a family effort." He placed a hand on her elbow and guided her along a path of stepping-stones. "Let's go around to the back of the building. When you were here for the reunion party, did you see that portion of the grounds?"

"Only a glimpse. That night was rather cool and windy. Most everyone preferred to stay inside. Where the wine was flowing. Along with all the good food," she added impishly.

"Then you might be surprised at what you see today. In my opinion, the back area is the best part of the place."

They walked side by side to the corner of the building, then made a sharp left. Savannah instantly stopped in her tracks and gasped at the sight before her.

"Oh, my. I don't recall anything looking this incredible!" she exclaimed.

"In the past few months, we've made a few additions and changes. There's always someone in the family coming up with new ideas to make the place more appealing to customers."

Moving forward, Savannah walked among a grouping of intricately carved sculptures posed upon an immaculate carpet of St. Augustine grass. One in particular, a cavalry officer mounted on a horse, caught her immediate attention. Along with a frontier woman holding the hand of a small boy. Nearby, a Spanish-tiled fountain added the tinkling sound of moving water to the chatter of the mockingbirds flitting among the tree limbs.

"We added the fountain a little over a year ago," Chaz told her as they walked slowly through the garden of statues. "And we change the sculptures with the seasons so that it gives visitors a change of scenery throughout the year."

Savannah looked past a charming statuette of hugging cherubs to see splashes of red, pink, yellow and white blossoms among a wave of greenery. "Is that a rose garden? I don't recall seeing it when I was here."

"It is a rose garden," he confirmed. "Here lately, the weather has been perfect for roses, so they're looking their best right now. And we've planted more shrubs and flowers around the grounds. The azaleas were exceptionally pretty this spring, but most of their blooms are gone now. Sorry, there aren't any camellias."

So he remembered that she liked camellias. Was that a part of a bodyguard's job?

Oh, Savanna, quit analyzing the man's every expression, every word. None of it means anything. He's only making conversation and attempting to make an awkward situation more bearable. You need to do the same.

Shoving away the reproving voice in her head, she smiled at him. "It's too warm for camellias to bloom now. But they would add some nice color in the cooler months."

Their slow stroll eventually took them to the roses and as they grew closer, she caught a whiff of the delicate fragrance drifting on the late morning air. Bending at the waist, she sniffed at one of the pink half-opened buds. "Mmm. These smell heavenly. Like being transported to a fairyland."

He responded by reaching over and snapping off a long-stemmed pink rose. Handing it to her, he said, "Now you can take the fragrance with you."

Did this man realize he'd just done a very romantic thing for her? Or was pinching off a rose and handing it to a woman just a casual occurrence for him? Either way, the gesture felt like he'd just kissed her on the cheek.

"Thank you, Chaz," she murmured.

"The rose—uh—matches your dress."

So why was he looking straight at her lips rather than her dress? Had he noticed the dusky pink lipstick she'd swiped on before they'd left the apartment? No! Her imagination was starting to run away with her. All these silly thoughts about kisses and lips were way out of her character. She didn't know where they were coming from or why. The man was her protector. To him, she was a job and nothing more.

"Hey, Chaz," a male voice suddenly called out.

Savannah looked around to see the man she remembered as Schuyler's husband walking toward them. Tall and dark, he didn't possess the same muscular build as Chaz, but there was a faint resemblance in their features.

"Carlo. How's it going this morning?"

Carlo gave his brother's shoulder an affectionate slap. "Great. We sold several cases of wine last night and took orders for at least a dozen more. We're planning to ship those out tomorrow."

"Sounds like things were hopping. I didn't realize you were putting on a tasting party last night," Chaz said.

"A food service convention was going on in the city," Carlo explained, his gaze settling curiously on Savanna. "Schuyler managed to get us an invitation and it paid off."

At that moment, Chaz wrapped a hand around Savannah's elbow and urged her forward. "Savannah, this is my brother Carlo. I think you two have met before."

"We have?" Carlo asked, then grinned and reached to shake her hand. "Only kidding, Savannah. I do remember you being at the reunion party. Along with the rest of your siblings."

Savannah smiled back at him, while thinking Carlo's outgoing personality was much different than Chaz's reserved nature. "I'm impressed that you remember me," she admitted. "There are so many of us New Orleans Fortunes."

"Believe me, Schuyler is excited about her new cousin being in Austin. You can be sure she'll be contacting you soon."

"It will be nice to see Schuyler again. Your wife is a lovely person. And very brave," Savannah added with a little laugh, "to try to get all of us Fortunes together in one spot."

Carlo chuckled. "My wife isn't just brave. She's fierce."

"She has to be to live with my brother," Chaz spoke up.

Surprised by his dry humor, Savannah glanced at him. Other than a faint dimple in one cheek, his expression was unchanged. Which made her wonder even more what was going on behind that handsome face.

"That's the truth." Carlo chuckled again before he turned a welcoming smile on Savannah. "I'm glad to see Chaz brought you along this morning. Hopefully, you'll enjoy seeing the winery again."

She cast another brief glance at Chaz before she turned a smile on Carlo. "Thank you, Carlo. I'm glad I came, too. Even though I'm here because Chaz doesn't want to take his eyes off me," she said, then realizing how suggestive that sounded, she quickly added, "Uh—I mean for safety reasons."

Carlo's grin deepened and Savannah wished she could kick herself for not phrasing her words more carefully.

"Chaz is very dedicated to his profession," Carlo reasoned. "Sometimes he can go overboard with safety precautions. But we love how he keeps everything protected."

The sound of a door opening and closing had all three of them glancing toward the building.

"There's Dad," Chaz announced. "He's come out to see what's going on."

As Savannah watched Chaz and Carlo's father stride purposely toward them, she gauged the man to be somewhere in his early sixties. A pair of dark trousers and a pale blue shirt left open at the throat covered his tall frame, while thick salt-and-pepper hair was combed straight back from his face to eventually fall below the collar of his shirt. A smile flashed white against his dark complexion.

"I should've known it was a beautiful woman keeping my sons occupied." His brown eyes scanned Savannah's face, then landed on Chaz. "Don't you think you should introduce me?"

"Give me time, Dad," Chaz told him.

Suddenly, Chaz's hand settled against the small of her back and though she tried not to read anything into the contact, it made her feel totally connected to this man at her side.

"Savannah, this is my father, Esteban Mendoza," Chaz spoke. "And, Dad, this is Miss Savannah Fortune from New Orleans."

Smiling at the older man, Savannah offered him her hand. He promptly lifted the back of it to his lips.

"I'm totally charmed to meet you, Miss Fortune. And how nice that you've come to visit Mendoza Winery. Will you be staying in Austin long?"

"For several weeks," she explained. "I'm a graduate student and here to do a research study at the university."

"Beauty and brains. That's very impressive." Esteban's eyes twinkled with appreciation, before he turned a more serious gaze on his son. "I'm surprised you accepted the job of guarding a woman. You've never been a bodyguard to a woman before."

"This was different. It involved the Fortune family and since I have many relatives married to Fortunes, I didn't want to refuse the job," Chaz explained.

Savannah got the impression Chaz was a bit uncomfortable discussing his bodyguard work with his father. Perhaps that was because it was something that took him away from the family business and he felt guilty about it, she thought. Or it could be that he and his father didn't always see eye-to-eye.

Frowning thoughtfully, Esteban looked at Savannah with a measure of concern. "Are you worried about your safety here in Austin, Miss Fortune?"

"Not exactly," she answered. "But my father is concerned. Chaz is working for him. Not me."

"Dad, Gerald Robinson is Savannah's uncle," Chaz explained. "I'm sure you've not forgotten the arson that occurred on his estate or how seriously Ben was injured. Miles Fortune, Savannah's father, is worried that he and his family have become targets. Especially here in Austin."

"Oh, I can understand someone going after Gerald. There's no doubt he's made enemies over the years. But who would possibly want to hurt a pretty little thing like Savannah? It doesn't make sense."

"That's exactly what I told my father, Mr. Mendoza," Savannah responded to Esteban. "Unfortunately, he doesn't view the situation like you do."

Esteban gave her a wide smile. "Well, if you were my daughter, I would see the situation differently, too. I would probably hire two bodyguards to keep you safe."

Carlo chuckled. "So the bodyguards could keep an eye on each other? Dad, your mind will never lose its naughty streak."

"I hope not," Esteban said with a laugh, then purposely glanced at his wristwatch. "You three are going to have to excuse me. I have a luncheon meeting in the next half hour."

"It was nice meeting you, Mr. Mendoza," Savannah told him.

"I hope we meet again soon, Miss Fortune. And see that you take proper care of her, Chaz," he said to his son.

Esteban strode off toward a black car parked a few feet away from Chaz's. As she thoughtfully watched him go, she said, "You two have a charming father."

Chaz groaned, while Carlo said with a chuckle, "That's what all the women say."

"Too many women," Chaz muttered.

Savannah wondered what that comment could possibly mean, when the hand that had been resting against her back all this time suddenly nudged her forward.

"If you've seen enough out here, let's go inside."

"Sure," she said to Chaz, then glanced at Carlo. "Will you join us?"

"Sorry. Chaz is going to have to be your official guide this morning. Schuyler is expecting me back home. I don't want to disappoint her."

"Certainly not. Please tell her hello for me."

"Will do." He looked at Chaz. "I'll call you later. We need to talk about the nightclub."

"Any time," Chaz told him.

Carlo hurried away and the two of them walked on to the building. After he punched in a code to allow them entrance, they walked down a hallway to a wide door that required another passcode to enter.

Curious about the extra security, she said, "There must be something top secret behind this door."

He glanced at her, his expression sober. "You could call it top secret. This is where Mendoza wine is made. No one outside the family is allowed back here without supervision. The blends for each label often change, but the notes for each wine are kept in a safe in the main office. Only immediate family members are privy to the combination of the safe."

"Wow. You're not taking any chances, are you?"

His lips took on a wry twist. "I don't take chances. Unless I'm forced to."

He pushed open the door and ushered her into a large area with a cement floor and a high open ceiling. A row of tall stainless steel fermenting tanks lined one side of the room, while the opposite side was equipped with a long chute-like conveyer, along with huge tubs and tables for washing and sorting the grapes.

Gazing curiously around her, she said, "I know next to nothing about wine-making, so this question is probably going to sound stupid, but I'll ask anyway. Is anything in the tanks right now? And when does it go from here to an aging barrel?"

"There's no fruit fermenting now. The new crop of grapes won't be harvested until late July or down into August. Depending on the weather. That's when this area of the winery gets extremely busy. The fermenting process usually takes about ten days and then it goes into barrels. From there, the time depends on the type of wine being made. Naturally, the longer it ages, the more expensive it gets."

"Yes, that part I do understand." She flashed him a smile. "My studies have taught me that reaching your goals takes time. And patience."

One of his dark brows arched upward. "And you have both?"

She laughed softly. No doubt, he was remembering the stubborn fight she put up yesterday when she'd learned her father had hired him as her bodyguard. "Well, I admit I need to work on the patience part."

A faint smile crossed his face. "We all need to work on that."

He gently cupped a hand around her elbow and urged her forward. His touch caused a fiery sensation to shoot up and down her arm and though her brain told her to step away from the temptation, she remained at his side and wondered once again what it was about this man that constantly reminded her that she was a woman.

The two of them ambled through the work area until they reached a set of large double doors. Chaz opened the one on the right and as Savannah stepped through the opening, she spotted hundreds of wooden barrels stored on racks that reached almost to the ceiling.

After he'd shown her the bottling area, they walked back down the hallway where they'd originally entered the building. Along the way, Chaz explained how the grapes were harvested by hand and was something that had to be done quickly and at exactly the right time to get the perfect flavor of the fruit. A part of Savannah's brain was listening intently, while the other part was registering the grace and strength of his body, the seductive scent emanating from his shirt and the way his black hair glistened beneath the overhead lighting. Just being near the man fractured her common sense.

Near the end of the hallway, they reached a rough-hewn wooden door with a sign that read Tasting Room.

Chaz grabbed the brass handle and after pulling the door wide, gestured for her to precede him into the open reception area. "We might as well be the first to visit the tasting room today," he said.

The huge room was much like Savannah remembered from the night of the Fortune reunion party. High-vaulted ceilings were supported by dark wooden beams, while ceramic tile in a pattern of dark blues and greens covered the floor. To one side was a long marble-topped bar where a few wine bottles, each with a different label, sat ready for customers to sample. Behind the bar, cushioned racks held more bottles. A few feet away, several small square tables made of dark wood and matching carved chairs were grouped near a wall painted with a mural of a sunny vineyard.

"Will the winery be open later today?"

"The Sunday hours are one o'clock to seven. Weekdays we open at noon and close at eight. The servers will be arriving soon to get everything ready."

She trailed a hand over the marble surface of the bar, then moseyed toward one of the tables.

Following a few steps behind her, he said, "Before I took you on a tour of the place I should've asked whether you like to drink wine. If you don't, that's perfectly fine. I have some friends who can't stand the stuff. They prefer a cold beer. Or a shot of bourbon, or scotch."

"I don't drink much alcohol of any sort," she admitted. "But my parents always have wine with dinner. Sometimes I have a glass with my family. I honestly know nothing about the different labels or taste. All I can tell you is that my parents buy very expensive bottles. Perhaps they've had Mendoza wine."

"Possibly. But now that you're here, you're welcome to try a glass," he suggested.

He was far more potent than a glass of wine, she thought. Put the two together and her head would definitely be swimming. Yet, she didn't want to disappoint him by declining his offer.

"I'd like that," she told him. "If you'll pick it out for me."

"My pleasure."

While he went after the wine, she seated herself at one of the tables. Moments later, he arrived carrying a tray loaded with two glasses, a tall green bottle and a small plate of neatly arranged fruits and cheeses.

As he placed everything on the table, she remarked, "Oh, I didn't realize you serve food here at the tasting room, too."

"We don't. This is something we keep around for ourselves and the staff." He seated himself directly across the table from her, then uncorked the bottle and poured a small amount of wine into each glass. "This has a sweet and fruity taste. Since you like sugary cereal, I thought you might prefer it."

First the camellias and now the cereal she'd eaten for breakfast. What else had Chaz noticed about her? That she was having trouble keeping her eyes off him? Had he already figured out that she was totally lost and insecure when it came down to developing a relationship with a man?

Trying to ignore those unsettling questions, she turned her attention to the wine and after giving it an appreciative sniff, she took a short sip. All the while, she was desperately aware of his dreamy brown eyes watching and waiting for her reaction.

Her cheeks warm, she stared at the pink tinged liquid in her glass. "Mmm. This is very good. And sweet."

"I'm glad you like it. I'll be sure to let my cousin Alejandro know. This blend is one that he specially crafted for his wife, Olivia—another Fortune woman, by the way."

What was it about all the marriages connecting the two families? Savannah wondered. Did mixing Mendozas and Fortunes create some sort of hypnotic spell or fiery chemistry? Maybe that had happened with a few family members, she surmised. But it was more than clear to Savannah that Chaz's senses hadn't fallen under any type of romantic enchantment. At least, not toward her. Sure, he'd given her the rose. But that had been nothing more than a polite gesture. He'd certainly not had the kind of twinkle in his eye that Esteban had when he'd kissed the back of her hand.

"Olivia and Alejandro," she repeated the names as she tried to match them to faces she'd met during her prior visit to Austin. "You're talking about Olivia Fortune Robinson, Gerald's daughter?"

"That's right. She and Alejandro are married and live here in Austin."

She nodded. "Yes, I recall. If I met your cousin Alejandro, I'm not remembering him. But like I said, my brief time here in Austin was one big whirlwind." She took another sip, then reached for a thin sliver of cheese. "How did your family get into the wine business? Did your father start all this?"

The corners of his mouth turned slightly downward, and she suddenly wondered how close Chaz actually was to his father and brothers. He'd said he'd moved here to

Austin to be with them. Surely that meant they were all a tight group. But that didn't necessarily mean everything was always hunky-dory between them, she surmised. There were times when things could get darned strained between her and her family.

"Alejandro is the reason the Mendozas are in the wine business. It began years ago with his working at a wine bar in South Beach. He took the job to help put himself through college and the experience motivated him to change his major to one that would educate him for a career in the wine industry. He's the one who actually purchased the winery, then convinced the rest of the family to join him."

"South Beach," she repeated. "Alejandro wasn't originally from Austin?"

"No. He and my father and all of us cousins lived in Miami before we migrated to Texas."

She regarded him thoughtfully. "I wondered why you didn't have much of a Texas twang. Do you still have relatives back in Miami?"

"Uncle Enrique and his five children live there."

He lifted the wineglass to his lips and beneath her lowered lashes, Savannah watched his bicep stretch the sleeve of his polo shirt to the extreme limit. Where did all those muscles come from? Most men would have to work out for hours every day in the gym to be as buff as Chaz. If he had a routine exercise regimen, he hadn't mentioned it. Which had her wondering if he was just one of those guys who didn't have to work at being fit. He was just naturally a hunk of sexy strength.

She drew in a deep breath, then slowly released it. "You Mendozas have a big family. Kind of like the Fortunes."

He made a sound that was something close to a snort. "There is no other family like the Fortunes."

His comment had her sitting just a bit straighter in her chair. "I hope you're not lumping the New Orleans Fortunes with those who are scattered across Texas. You might not believe it, but my father is nothing like Gerald Robinson. He hasn't sired a bunch of illegitimate children or had a series of adulterous affairs. My mother isn't secretly plotting revenge or hell bent on harming people she's never even met!"

A half grin suddenly curved his lips. "Whew! Glad you got that off your chest?"

She could see he was joking, which made her even more aware of her defensive rant. "Sorry, Chaz. I didn't intend to get carried away. It's just that I'm learning that being connected to this set of Texas Fortunes is not all sunshine and lollipops."

"No need for you to be so defensive. I wasn't referring to your branch of the family. It's Gerald and his ex that are causing all the worries."

She swished the wine around in her goblet, while wondering exactly how much Chaz knew about the Fortunes here in Austin. Enough for him to figure out that they had as many problems as they had thousand-dollar bills. And that was more than any one person could count.

Sighing, she said, "When Dad first learned that he and Gerald had the same father, he wanted the truth of the matter kept under wraps. No one in the family was to breathe a word about any of it. He kept pounding out the fact that the New Orleans Fortunes were nothing like Gerald Robinson and his branch of the Fortunes. Our reputation was untarnished, but it would hardly stay that way if people learned we were related to Gerald."

"But somehow the information about Miles and Gerald got out anyway."

Besides Kenneth and Gerald, her father had also discovered he had two more Fortune brothers, Gary and David, both of whom lived far away from Texas. Could be that Chaz had already learned that particular information through his sister-in-law, Schuyler, or maybe he hadn't. Either way, Savannah wasn't going to go into those details with Chaz. The situation was already awkward enough without adding to it.

She nodded. "Secrets have a way of getting out. And because the family connection was revealed, you're now a bodyguard to a graduate student. Simply because she's Gerald Robinson's niece. It's crazy."

"In many ways, the Fortune wealth is toxic. It makes people crazy," he reasoned.

Glancing over the rim of her glass, she studied his face. "You make it sound like having money is more like a curse than a blessing."

"I didn't say that. I only meant that money makes puppets out of many people."

Savannah considered his remark before she eventually replied. "Hmm. I guess it's like those miners I talked about in the San Juans in the 1840s. Gold fever probably caused most of them to die either by the hand of someone else or the elements."

"Exactly. Money often makes people behave irrationally."

Well, she could've told him it wasn't money that was putting irrational thoughts in her head but rather his rugged presence. For her to be thinking how she'd like to kiss the wine off his lips was totally absurd.

He drained his glass and glanced at his watch. "If you're finished, I'm going to put these things away. Be-

fore the place gets busy, I need to check out a few things
in the office. It will only take a few minutes. Will you
be comfortable here?"

"If you don't mind, I think I'll wait for you out in the
garden."

"Fine," he replied. "I'll catch up with you there."

He gathered everything from the table and left the
tasting room. Once he was gone, Savannah picked up the
pink rose he'd given her and made her way back outside
to the sculpture garden.

The midday sun filtered through the trees to dapple
the ground and warm her bare shoulders. With no one
else around, the garden felt like a private haven, something she desperately needed at the moment. She longed
to escape this strange, unexpected reaction she was having to Chaz. She wanted to stop thinking about him. She
wanted to stop studying every little nuance of his features, his voice and rock-hard body. She needed to quit
fantasizing about touching him. Kissing him. Making
love to him. He was off-limits. Totally off-limits!

She meandered through the statues until she reached a
wrought-iron park bench positioned beneath the drooping
limbs of a live oak. Savannah took a seat on the bench
and as the soothing sound of the nearby fountain washed
over her, the image of the hugging cherubs caught her
attention.

For some inexplicable reason, the sweet innocence of
their intricately carved faces made her think of her late
friend, Bethann. She'd been like a sister to Savannah
and as they'd entered their teenage years together, they'd
planned, and hoped, and dreamed about their futures.
Bethann had been a true romantic in every sense of the
word and had insisted she'd be married before she was
twenty-five. Her wedding would be filled with flowers,

lace and candles, and she and her prince-charming husband would have at least four children. She'd dreamed of living in a beach house, where the children could play in the sand and swim, while she and her husband watched the sun set across the water.

But then Bethann had gotten sick with a rare lung disorder and Savannah had watched helplessly as her friend begin to wither away, until she'd finally lost the battle to live. Bethann's dream of having a prince charming and four children never had a chance to come true.

Since then, Savannah had focused her entire life on the science of diseases, always driven with the thought of sparing some other young person from Bethann's fate. During the many years of acquiring an education, Savannah had failed to meet her own prince charming, much less marry one. There were no children on the horizon or immediate plans to have a family of her own. What would Bethann think about her friend's loveless life? Would she appreciate the fact that Savanna's nights were spent with her arms wrapped around a theory book instead of a man?

Tears unexpectedly sprang to her eyes and before she could choke them back, she spotted Chaz's boots planted firmly in the grass in front of her.

Mortified that he'd caught her in such an emotional state, she quickly used the back of her hand to dash away the moisture on her cheeks.

"Savannah, are you—you're crying!"

Shaking her head, she stood and attempted to give him a bright smile. "I'm fine. Really. Are you ready to go?"

He didn't answer her with words. Instead, he reached out and pulled her close against him. The thought of resisting flashed through her mind. But it was nothing more than an empty notion, too weak to fight off the need to feel the comfort of his arms wrapped around her.

And as her cheek settled against the hard muscles of his chest, she realized that at some point from yesterday to this very moment, he'd become much more than her bodyguard.

Chapter Six

The next morning, Chaz sat behind the steering wheel of his car and checked his watch for the third time in the past fifteen minutes.

What the hell was he doing? Less than an hour had passed since he'd dropped off Savannah at the science laboratory where she'd be meeting with the study group. No doubt, she was already immersed in her work, her mind focused on unlocking the mystery of diseases. Whereas, he was sitting in his car, wondering how he was going to drive away and put her out of his mind. Even for ten minutes.

Damn it! Yesterday in the sculpture garden, he should've ignored the tears glittering on her cheeks. He should've dismissed the shadows in her hazel eyes and the quiver of her lips. But he'd been too weak to stand back and wait for her to compose herself. Too overcome with the need to comfort her. Touch her.

Hours had passed since then and he still couldn't push

the incident out of his mind. She'd felt so small and vulnerable in his arms, yet at the same time her soft curves had sparked his desire.

He'd desperately wanted to kiss her. He'd wanted to explore her lips and find out for himself if they tasted anything like the sweet womanly scent of her hair and skin. And if the sound of the workers arriving in the front of the building hadn't interrupted the moment, he probably would have kissed her. Or at least, attempted it.

What a hell of a mistake that would've been, he thought sickly. His whole reputation as a responsible bodyguard would have gone up in flames. Would a few moments of pleasure be worth the cost? No. Never. Allison had already taught him that rich girls were not his style. And a rich girl definitely wasn't in his future. Especially a petite brunette with the last name of Fortune.

Heaving out a long breath, he looked across the street to the block of buildings where Savannah would be doing most of her studying the next few weeks. A day before she'd arrived in Austin, Chaz had spoken with building security, along with the campus police about the safety protocols that were followed on the university. Chaz had been reassured by what he'd learned, yet it wasn't enough to make him feel completely comfortable about leaving her. But short of camping out in the hallway, there wasn't much more he could do. It wasn't feasible or reasonable to keep his eyes on her every second of the day. Furthermore, he shouldn't want to.

Muttering a curse under his breath, he started the car and jerked it into gear. Sitting here in the parking lot, fretting over the situation was futile.

All you have to do to get away from this anguish is to call Miles Fortune and tell him you're done. But no, you're too worried about some other guy moving into

Savannah's apartment. Some other guy holding her in his arms. And that's the real problem, isn't it?

Chaz was trying to ignore the nasty little voice going off in his head when his cell phone rang. He glanced at the screen in the middle of his dashboard and groaned out loud when he realized the caller was Miles Fortune.

In his present frame of mind, Savannah's father was the last person he should be talking to. But Miles had contracted Chaz's services and it was mandatory to keep communications open with a client.

Punching a button, Chaz relied on the hands-free connection to allow him to drive safely and talk at the same time. "Hello, Mr. Fortune."

The few times Chaz had talked with Miles, he'd gotten straight to the point and this morning was no different.

"Good morning, Mr. Mendoza. I'm checking to see if everything is going okay with Savannah."

Other than a brief crying spell and Chaz holding her as though she belonged to him, everything was great, he thought ruefully. To Miles, he said, "Your daughter is fine, sir. She's currently on campus and will be in class for most of the day."

"And where are you?" he asked abruptly. "I'm assuming you're in the building with her."

It was all Chaz could do to keep from cursing. When he'd first discussed this job with Miles Fortune, the man had seemed to understand the obstacles a bodyguard often encountered while trying to keep a constant watch over a person. At the time, he'd believed the man understood the situation and would be fairly reasonable to work for. Apparently, the fact that Savannah was hundreds of miles away and in the very heart of Charlotte's domain was making the multimillionaire banker more than anxious.

"Your assumption is wrong," Chaz told him. "I'm not in the building with Savannah. That's impossible."

"Mr. Mendoza, I told you—"

"No, Mr. Fortune," he purposely interrupted. "I told you from the very beginning that it would be impossible for me to physically be in your daughter's presence twenty-four hours a day. It's not my job to interrupt her life."

"It's damned well your job to protect her life! To hell with the interruption! She'll just have to deal with it."

Chaz was beginning to see that having Miles Fortune for a father had given Savannah plenty enough to deal with. The idea that this man wanted to keep his grown daughter tightly under his thumb, even if it was for the sake of her safety, made Chaz want to protect her even more.

"You're correct," Chaz replied. "It is my responsibility to make sure she remains safe and unharmed. I'm doing that to the best of my ability. If you feel like someone else could do a better job of it, then I won't hold you to our agreement."

Chaz hadn't meant to throw those last words at the man, but Miles Fortune's demanding attitude had struck a burning match to his already-short fuse.

Long moments of silence stretched inside the car and as Chaz deftly moved through the busy morning traffic of downtown Austin, he waited for Miles Fortune to tell him he was fired. The reality hit the pit of his stomach like a heavy rock. How was he going to explain this to Savannah? And how was she going to feel about it? Relieved? Happy?

Finally, Miles spoke, "I think we both need to take a deep breath and start over. You're right, Chaz. You are the bodyguard. You know more than I about the rules of what you can and can't do. If I seem anxious, it's because—well, I love my daughter very much. I realize she's twenty-five years old. But she's never been away from home. Not like this. And when I think about what Charlotte Robinson might be planning and plotting next, it's enough to make me drink a double scotch at eight o'clock in the morning."

Chaz was shocked that the man had relented. He was also extremely relieved. Which could only mean one thing: he was already getting far too attached to Savannah.

"I understand, sir. Your concerns are warranted. Have you gained any new information on Charlotte or her whereabouts?" Chaz asked as he braked the car to a halt behind a red light.

"Since Savannah arrived in Austin, I've spoken with Connor Fortunado. He and his operatives are working overtime, but so far they've had no luck in tracking her whereabouts. However, that detail is only a part of the problem. With Charlotte's money and connections, Connor feels certain she has her spies and thugs hanging around Austin. Which means danger could come in any shape or form."

"I understand," Chaz told him. "I'll see that your daughter doesn't unnecessarily expose herself to the risk."

"I'm counting on you," Miles replied, then awkwardly cleared his throat. "Can you tell me how she is otherwise? She was very angry with me when she left New Orleans."

Yesterday, in the sculpture garden when Chaz had held her in his arms, he'd not felt anger from her, only loss and sadness. Since then, Chaz hadn't questioned her about her tears and she'd not explained. Still, he felt sure her tears had been totally unrelated to her father.

"Savannah has accepted the fact that I'll be around. Whether she's still angry with you, I couldn't say."

Chaz could hear the man release a long breath.

"I'll just be glad when someone catches up to Charlotte Prendergast Robinson," Miles muttered. "Maybe then all of us Fortunes will get some relief."

Before Chaz could make any sort of reply, Miles explained he was heading into a ten o'clock meeting and abruptly ended the call.

Chaz made sure his phone was disconnected, then turned his attention back to the slow-moving traffic.

Relief? He didn't expect to find any until Savannah was safely back in New Orleans.

Inside a long room that served as a classroom and a working laboratory, Savannah sat at a desk, staring blankly at the problem she'd been trying to solve for the past half hour. Normally, actuary equations were a snap for Savannah to calculate. But this one had stumped her.

Face it, Savannah. You can't stop thinking about Chaz Mendoza. Every touch of his hand, every word from his lips is stuck in your brain. Daydreaming about your sexy bodyguard is going to put you on a fast downhill slide.

Savannah rubbed fingertips against her furrowed brow, while wishing she could push the reproachful voice straight out of her head. She didn't want to believe that she'd allowed herself to stray, if only for a few brief minutes, away from the path she'd chosen for herself. Yet, deep down, she recognized that for the first time in her life, she'd met up with something strong enough to disengage her thoughts from her studies. And she was furious with herself for being so sappy. So goofily romantic.

Chaz wasn't interested in her. And even if he were, nothing between them could last. As soon as her studies here at UT were over, she'd be going back to New Orleans. He'd be here in Austin working in his family's wine business. Those hard facts should have been enough to jerk her back to reality. But they weren't enough to erase the memory of how she'd felt having her cheek against his chest and the beat of his heart thumping in her ear. She could've stood there in his arms forever and died a happy woman.

"Miss Fortune, class is finished for the day. If you'd like to stay longer, I can advise security to lock up later— after you leave."

Savannah looked up to see the lab had emptied, except for Professor Barcroft, who was striding purposely toward her desk.

Short, with a barrel waist, a partially bald head and a stony face partly hidden behind a pair of bifocals, the man hardly looked like a genius or anything close to it. However, in the academic world, Professor Barcroft was revered among his peers, and students fought to get into his classes. The moment Savannah had learned he'd be heading up the study group, she felt like she'd won the lottery. Now, because of her inability to focus, she'd missed huge hunks of his lecture and squandered the first lesson.

"Oh. I'm sorry, Professor Barcroft. I hadn't realized so much time had passed. I was trying to use an actuarial equation to make my point." She placed the paper in his outstretched hand. "I'm sure you'll let me know if it's not correct."

The smile on his face was a bit ruthless and reminded Savannah of her father's expression when he issued a warning.

"The first day of the study can be jarring for some students," he said. "I'm sure by tomorrow you'll have yourself pulled together and ready to get down to work."

Savannah could feel a blush stealing across her face. Had this eagle-eyed professor caught her staring off into space? Damn Chaz Mendoza anyway! She'd worked very hard to get the invitation to this study group, and later on down the line, it would look highly impressive on a résumé. That is, if she didn't end up making herself look like an eighth-grade student rather than a college graduate.

"I assure you I'll be more than ready. Thank you, Professor." Snatching up her tote bag from beneath her desk, she jumped to her feet and hurried out of the laboratory.

At the end of a long hallway, she reached a set of exit doors where Chaz had promised he'd be waiting for her.

As soon as she stepped out of the building, she spotted him sitting on one of the park benches that bordered the sidewalk. The sight of him caused her heart to do a silly little flip and she suddenly wondered how it might feel to hurry to his side and throw her arms around his neck, as though he belonged to her and she belonged to him. But that sort of behavior wasn't really her style. She didn't want to cross any lines in this relationship, and besides, she was hardly the type to flirt so outrageously.

Long before Savannah reached the bench, he spotted her and after slipping the phone he'd been scanning into his shirt pocket, he rose and walked down the sidewalk to meet her.

"Hello," he greeted. "Are you finished for the day, or do you need to go somewhere else on campus?"

Why did her lips insist on tilting into a smile? Why did she want to hook her arm through his and snuggle herself to his side? Nothing about her strange reactions to the man made sense. Nor did she seem capable of stopping them.

"I'm finished," she told him. "Thank goodness."

He darted a glance at her. "Bad day?"

Bad? She supposed dreaming about him all day couldn't be described as bad. Just highly unsettling.

"No. Not really. The professor is new. The surroundings are different. It will take me a few days to get used to the change and get in the groove."

They began to walk side by side to the parking area some distance away. Savannah noticed that he'd changed from the khakis and polo shirt he'd been wearing that morning. Now a pair of faded blue jeans hugged his rear and clung to his muscled thighs, while an army-green T-shirt outlined every sinewy muscle of his upper body.

He asked, "You didn't have any problems?"

Before he'd left her this morning, he'd made sure she had her cell phone tucked inside her handbag and his number at the top of her contact list. If she had any sort of problem, either big or small, she was to call him. Did thinking about him for fifty-five minutes out of the hour constitute a problem?

"What sort of problems are you talking about?" she asked.

"Like anyone strange approaching you? Anyone questioning you about your family here in Austin or back in New Orleans?"

"No. Really, Chaz, do you honestly expect someone on campus to go to such lengths to try to harm me? I mean, it would be difficult to come up with the proper identification needed to get into the work lab."

"I wouldn't say that. Snakes have a way of slithering through the smallest of cracks. But I have to trust the security measures that the university has in place."

"Well, if it makes you feel any better, all of our classes will be held in the same room we were in today. So I won't be walking all over campus. The only other building I'll possibly visit is the library and it's not that far away."

He frowned and she started to ask him what was wrong, then quickly stopped herself. Yesterday, when they left the winery, his mood had turned dark and quiet and since then it hadn't appeared to improve. Meeting him only three days ago, it was impossible for Savannah to know if he was the type of guy that changed moods as often as the weather. But considering the timing, Savannah had to wonder if he regretted taking her to the winery and introducing her to his brother and father. Even worse, did he regret those moments in the sculpture garden when he'd held her close and stroked a hand over her hair?

But why would he? What was there to regret? She'd instantly dried her tears. She'd not made a blubbering fool of herself all over him. And once they'd left the winery, she'd not even mentioned the incident. Nor did she plan to.

"Just don't go to the library alone," he said bluntly. "Make sure you take someone that you trust with you."

"I will," she promised. "I met a nice lady from Beaumont in the study group. Since that's just a hop and a jump from New Orleans, we have a lot in common. Marva's in her sixties and finishing up her doctorate. Before her children grew up and left home, she only had a high school diploma. I'm so inspired by her spirit and determination. I can only hope I'll be that ambitious and productive when I reach that age."

He glanced at her. "You have plans to go for your doctorate?"

"Most definitely. The quicker, the better. Unless—"

His black brows formed a single line above his narrowed eyes. "Unless?"

"Uh—something causes me to pause my studies for a while." Like allowing herself to be a woman in every sense of the word. Allowing herself to indulge in a flirtation. In an attraction. The thoughts came out of nowhere, shocking her as they zinged through her head. That kind of thinking wasn't her! Not at all! "You know—things happen that are out of a person's control."

"Sure. I know."

The drive to Live Oak Lane was basically done in silence. Savannah got the impression that Chaz wanted to be left to his own thoughts—whatever they might be. Was there a woman somewhere in the city that he was wishing he could visit? Perhaps even spend the night with? If so, then being Savannah's bodyguard was putting a cramp in his love life.

The notion left her feeling like a bit of a nuisance and lonelier than she could ever remember being. But that was only because she was away from home and missing the company of her family, she assured herself. She didn't need to make chitchat with Chaz. She didn't care if he preferred to keep his thoughts to himself. The less she connected with him, the better off she'd be today, tomorrow and every day after that.

As soon they arrived at the apartment, Savannah went straight to her bedroom. After changing clothes, she gathered up the notes she'd managed to jot down during class and curled up in a chair. She remained there, doing her best to focus on Professor Barcroft's remarks, until hunger eventually drove her to the kitchen.

When she walked into the room, she was surprised to find Chaz standing at the gas range stirring something in a large skillet. The delicious aroma of cooking food permeated the air and caused her mouth to water.

"Mmm. Something smells yummy." In spite of vow-ing to keep her distance from him, she walked over to the range and stood next to him. "You didn't tell me you could cook."

"You didn't ask."

"What is that?" She peered closer at the frying mixture in the skillet. "It looks like fish with a bunch of other things."

"It's some of the fish you purchased during your grocery shopping binge. The rest is tomatoes, onions and two kinds of peppers. Bell for flavor and jalapeño for heat."

He picked up a bottle of soy sauce and doused the whole thing. Her empty stomach growled.

"Where did you learn to do this? Surely not in the army."

He slanted her a dry look. "Soldiers have to eat, too. But no, my KP duties were limited to washing dishes and mopping floors. The cooking is a family thing. All of us brothers are fairly handy in the kitchen."

Ever since Chaz had picked her up at the university, she'd been trying to convince herself that she didn't want to talk to him. That she didn't need or want his company. But she'd only been fooling herself. "Cooking is something that interested all of you?"

"Hmm. I guess you could say we learned out of necessity more than interest."

She wanted to ask him what he meant by that remark, but decided he probably wouldn't want to answer. After meeting his father and brother yesterday, many questions about his family had crossed her mind. Such as the whereabouts of his mother and why he never mentioned her. But that, too, was none of her business.

No, she'd keep the questions to herself, she decided. And maybe a time would come when Chaz would want to talk to her about the parts of his life that mattered the most.

"Uh, were you planning on sharing your meal?" she dared to ask "Or is all of that for you?"

He turned his head toward her and she found herself looking into chocolate-brown eyes veiled with thick black lashes. Sensual bedroom eyes. She'd heard of them, but had never seen them. Until she'd met this man.

He turned his attention back to the skillet. "I believe there's enough here for the both of us. That is, if you trust my cooking."

"If the aroma coming from that skillet is anything like the taste, I don't think I'll have any trouble choking it down," she said impishly, then asked, "Is there anything I can do?"

"You can set the table and get us something to drink. The iced tea you made yesterday would be good," he suggested. "If there's any left."

"There's plenty of tea," she told him. "I'll get it and the table ready."

Leaving his side, she went to work gathering glasses, plates and utensils. "Would you rather eat here in the kitchen," she asked, "or in the dining room?"

"Wherever," he answered as he continued to stir the fish and vegetables. "I'm sure you'd prefer the dining room."

"Wrong. I like it here in the kitchen. We can see out the glass doors to the patio."

"Those sliding glass doors are a security nightmare," he said gruffly. "If you ever get that house you want on Bourbon Street, make sure it doesn't have any."

Did he view everything with security in mind? Or did he think because she was a Fortune she was always going to be in danger? Dear God, she certainly hoped that wasn't the case.

"I'll keep that in mind, Chaz."

She took her time setting the table with plates, glasses, linen napkins and silverware, then stood back to survey her work. Everything looked nice, yet the table needed something more.

"Flowers," she said, more to herself than to him. "That's the only thing missing."

But she wasn't back home in the Garden District where she could walk outside to her mother's flower beds and cut whatever she wanted. There were a few blooming shrubs in front of the apartment, but those were oleanders and she hardly wanted to put anything toxic on the dinner table.

The rose! *Her* rose!

She hurried out of the kitchen and returned moments later with a juice glass partially filled with water and the pink rose bud. After placing it in the middle of the small table, she stood back and smiled.

"It's perfect now."

"This isn't a dinner party, Savannah."

The flat remark had her glancing over her shoulder to see he was looking at her, and the scowl on his face was like a storm cloud blocking out the sun.

"What is that supposed to mean?"

"You're taking pains with the table like you're expecting guests."

"We're having dinner," she said primly. "Not eating a hot dog at the fair."

The roll of his eyes was even worse than his scowl and Savannah had to fight the unladylike urge to march over and kick his shin.

"Don't tell me you've done something as improper as

eating something with your hands while walking around a dusty midway. I can't imagine it, Miss Fortune."

The sarcasm in his voice, especially the way he'd spoken her name, should have sent her temper skyrocketing. Instead, it hurt to think he viewed her as a spoiled diva. She wasn't that sort of person.

With a shake of her head, she said, "You don't understand, Chaz. I—uh, never get to do this sort of thing at my parents' home, so it's fun for me. And since you've done all the cooking, I want to make the table look nice for you."

His expression stoic, he studied her for a brief moment, then turned back to the stove. "Fine," he said curtly. "This is your apartment. Not mine."

She pressed her lips tightly together. Calling him a jerk wouldn't fix anything. "That's right," she said. "But thanks to my father, you and I are sharing this living space."

"I guess you think it's my fault that you're a Fortune— that you need protecting."

She needed protection all right, Savannah thought ruefully. The kind that would keep her feelings all safely wrapped away from Chaz Mendoza.

With a heavy sigh, she pulled a plastic pitcher from the refrigerator. "I'm sorry that living here with me is putting you under such a strain, Chaz. Really, I am. I understand that you have a life of your own. It can't be easy to give up your friends and social life for an extended period of time."

He didn't make any sort of reply. Which didn't surprise Savannah. He only talked when the mood struck him. And even then, she never knew what to expect. One minute he was sweet as sugar, the next as bitter as green persimmon.

Back at the table, she was pouring tea into ice-filled glasses and wondering if she should find some excuse to forgo this impromptu dinner, when he suddenly appeared beside her.

She turned her head just enough to see his brooding face and that was all it took to make her heart leap into her throat. Her grip on the pitcher wavered and she placed it on the tabletop rather than risk spilling the tea everywhere.

To her further dismay, he wrapped a hand around her upper arm. The sensation of his long fingers pressing into her flesh left her feeling like a meek little mouse caught in a hawk's talons.

"You don't understand anything about me," he said gruffly. "You don't even know me."

She dared to meet his gaze and as she looked deep into the brown depths of his eyes, she saw shadows. The kind that harbored anger, loss and pain. Had he endured some sort of tragedy? Something in the army? Something about his family?

All at once, Savannah recognized there was a soft, vulnerable place inside of him, a space he didn't want anyone else to see. Especially her. The realization was all it took to put a lump in her throat and a wobbly smile on her face.

"You don't know anything about me, either," she murmured.

Suddenly, the shadows in his eyes were replaced with a warm flickering light and then his gaze dropped to her lips. Raw energy crackled between them and Savannah was certain all the oxygen was being sucked from her lungs. Was he actually going to kiss her?

Her legs began to tremble and the hold he had on her arm had turned to a band of fire circling her flesh. She felt her upper body gravitating toward his. Or was the weakness in her knees causing her to sway?

Either way, she was certain she was going to wilt and she latched a hand onto the edge of the table and drew in a shaky breath.

"You're right," he said, his voice husky. "We don't really know each other. But I—"

"Yes?"

His gaze slowly lifted back to hers and she could see the beckoning light in his eyes had vanished and the tense moment between them was over. She didn't know whether to be disappointed or relieved.

"I think we'd better eat now." He cleared his throat and added, "Before the food gets cold."

"Yes, I'm hungry."

She was hungry for him, Savannah thought. And all the things she'd missed since she'd grown into womanhood.

But he was her bodyguard and the moment she headed back to New Orleans, his services would end. He'd go back to his life and she'd return to hers.

She'd defied her father and made this trip to Austin anyway. Because she'd believed her stint at the university would be a big boon to her education and a favorable mark for any future employer to see. But at some point during these past few days, those things had lost their importance. Now she was more concerned with holding on to her heart.

Chapter Seven

After dinner, Chaz loaded the dishwasher, while Savannah made coffee and dished up servings of coconut cake she'd purchased from the bakery. He didn't really want to eat dessert. But he'd found it impossible to tell her no. Just like it had been impossible to keep his eyes off her during dinner.

Just how was a man supposed to ignore the lovely image she made with her hair pulled into a messy knot on the top of her head, the straps of a red tank top falling off her shoulders and her creamy skin glowing beneath the soft light hanging over the kitchen table?

And that damned rose! Giving it to her hadn't been a deliberate romantic gesture, he mentally argued. The whole thing had been an impulsive reaction to the pleasure she was displaying over the rose garden. Nothing more. Nothing less. He sure as hell hadn't expected her to keep the flower. In fact, after the two of them had returned from the winery, Chaz hadn't seen the rose again,

"4 for 4" MINI-SURVEY

We are prepared to **REWARD** you with 2 FREE books and 2 FREE gifts for completing our MINI SURVEY!

FREE
Value Over
$20!

You'll get...

TWO FREE BOOKS & TWO FREE GIFTS

just for participating in our Mini Survey!

Dear Reader,

IT'S A FACT: if you answer 4 quick questions, we'll send you 4 FREE REWARDS!

I'm not kidding you. As a leading publisher of women's fiction, we value your opinions… and your time. That's why we are prepared to **reward** you handsomely for completing our mini-survey. In fact, we have 4 Free Rewards for you, including 2 free books and 2 free gifts.

As you may have guessed, that's why our mini-survey is called **"4 for 4".** Answer 4 questions and get 4 Free Rewards. It's that simple!

Thank you for participating in our survey,

Pam Powers

To get your 4 FREE REWARDS:
Complete the survey below and return the insert today to receive 2 FREE BOOKS and 2 FREE GIFTS guaranteed!

"4 for 4" MINI-SURVEY

1 Is reading one of your favorite hobbies?
　　　　☐ YES　　　☐ NO

2 Do you prefer to read instead of watch TV?
　　　　☐ YES　　　☐ NO

3 Do you read newspapers and magazines?
　　　　☐ YES　　　☐ NO

4 Do you enjoy trying new book series with FREE BOOKS?
　　　　☐ YES　　　☐ NO

YES! I have completed the above Mini-Survey. Please send me my 4 FREE REWARDS (worth over $20 retail). I understand that I am under no obligation to buy anything, as explained on the back of this card.

235/235 HDL GNRV

FIRST NAME	LAST NAME

ADDRESS

APT.#	CITY

STATE/PROV.	ZIP/POSTAL CODE

READER SERVICE—Here's how it works:

▼ If offer card is missing write to: Reader Service, P.O. Box 1341, Buffalo, NY 14240-8531 or visit www.ReaderService.com ▼

BUSINESS REPLY MAIL
FIRST-CLASS MAIL   PERMIT NO. 717   BUFFALO, NY

POSTAGE WILL BE PAID BY ADDRESSEE

READER SERVICE
PO BOX 1341
BUFFALO NY 14240-8571

NO POSTAGE
NECESSARY
IF MAILED
IN THE
UNITED STATES

so he'd assumed she'd tossed the flower into the trash. He'd never imagined she'd put the thing in water and carry it to her bedroom.

What did that mean anyway? That she simply liked roses? Or had she especially liked this one because he'd given it to her?

Hell, Chaz, what are you thinking? Savannah is a Fortune. She can buy all the roses she wants, anytime she wants. And if she doesn't want to buy them for herself, there are plenty of men around who'd be more than happy to give her dozens of the things. One little bud from the winery garden doesn't mean anything special to her. You don't mean anything special to her.

"I'm going to take my cake and coffee out to the patio," she said. "Want to join me?"

Her question jarred him from his tumultuous thoughts and he looked beyond her to the patio doors. It was dark now and the evening breeze would be just about perfect, Chaz thought. But sitting out under the moon and stars with Savannah wasn't a smart thing to do. Not when it was all he could do to keep his hands to himself and his mind on something other than kissing her.

He must have hesitated about answering longer than he thought, because she suddenly said, "If you'd rather not, that's fine with me. I don't think there's any chance of someone scaling the privacy fence and snatching me away."

The teasing tone in her voice told Chaz she didn't have a clue as to how much he actually worried about her safety. And maybe that was for the best. As a bodyguard, he wasn't supposed to be this obsessed with his client.

Hoping he looked more like a cool cat instead of a sick calf, he said, "I'll join you."

With a coffee mug in one hand and a dessert plate in

the other, she headed out the patio doors. Chaz followed after her and tried not to notice the sway of her hips beneath the long soft skirt she was wearing.

"Oh, the breeze feels lovely." She eased down in the glider and balanced the cake on her knees. "After being cooped up in the lab all day, it's nice to be outdoors."

He took a seat in the chair across from her. "The heat hasn't hit Austin yet. You'll probably be back in New Orleans before it reaches sweltering temperatures."

She didn't say anything to that and he turned his attention to eating the cake. He didn't want to think about her leaving. He didn't want to think about tomorrow. All he wanted to think about was sitting here in the dark. With her.

After a few moments, she set her plate aside and looked at him. Chaz looked back and wondered how she would react if he moved across the short space between them and pulled her into his arms. Would her soft cheek nestle against his chest as it had yesterday? Or would she pull away and remind him that he was supposed to be guarding, not touching?

"Chaz, I think there's something I should explain about—well, about yesterday. In the winery garden."

What was going on here? Was she reading his mind?

"There's nothing to explain."

She smoothed a hand over her skirt and as Chaz watched her, he couldn't recall ever knowing a woman who looked as feminine as she did or moved with such grace.

"Yes. I believe there is. Because it seems to me that ever since we left the winery you've been upset with me."

Something twisted in the middle of his chest.

"I've not been upset."

Which was true, Chaz thought. If he'd appeared angry,

it was because he'd been fighting like hell to hold on to his senses—and keep his hands off her. But more than anything, he'd been trying to convince himself that, for a guy like him, she was as reachable as the evening stars.

"Okay. But I want to explain anyway," she told him. "Just so you'll know I'm not a woman who goes around crying over a hangnail or weeps because she's lost her favorite tube of lipstick."

"Before you arrived in Austin, I might have imagined you as that sort. But not now."

Her sigh was a wistful sound and before he could stop himself, he was sitting next to her on the glider with his hand tightly curled around hers.

"Savannah, this isn't necessary. I understand. You had a melancholy moment. We all have them at one time or another."

The look in her eyes was warm and appreciative.

"Yes, and some of us have more of those moments than others. Thankfully, mine are getting few and far between. But yesterday one of the statues in the garden got me to thinking about someone I had loved very much. She died almost ten years ago."

He didn't want to be drawn into her joys or sorrows. He didn't want to be sucked into her life, only to have her jerk it all away. The same way Allison had taken away every dream he'd had for the future. Their future.

And yet, Chaz couldn't force himself to leave her side. Not with the plaintive look in her eyes tying knots in his stomach. Not with her soft fingers twining around his.

"She?" he asked her.

Nodding, she said, "Her name was Bethann. From the time we were five years old, we attended the same elementary school—a private school for girls. Although we were opposite in looks and personality, we were closer than most sisters. Blonde and blue-eyed, she had a smile that dazzled. She was quite an athlete and would've certainly lettered in softball and basketball if—"

She looked toward the dark shadows of the yard and swallowed, and Chaz realized he was seeing Savannah in a way he had never expected. He was seeing that having a powerful father and an impressive last name hadn't necessarily made her world perfect.

The awkward moment stretched until he asked, "What happened to your friend? Car accident?"

She turned back to him and as the moonlight dappled her face, he could see her expression was stark and still, as though she were purposely trying to keep her emotions hidden from him.

Because she believes it annoys you to see her feelings. Because she thinks you regret holding her. Consoling her.

The thoughts circling through his head left a sick feeling in the pit of his stomach. He didn't want Savannah to feel as though she needed to hide from him.

Shaking her head, she said, "A quick accident would've been more merciful than what Bethann went through. When she began having breathing problems, she was initially diagnosed with asthma. But when the treatment for that failed to help, the doctors discovered she had a rare lung disease."

"Obviously, it wasn't curable."

She pulled in a deep breath, then heaved it out. "No. But for a few years, it was treatable. Until the meds quit making a difference. She spent her fifteenth birthday in a hospital hooked up to tubes and machines. She died a few days afterward."

"And you were crushed."

Nodding, she said, "Bethann was so sweet, and pretty, and funny. And emotionally strong. She faced death like another adventure to be met. During that time, my parents kept reminding me that Bethann was no longer suffering. But that was little comfort to a fifteen-year-old girl who'd lost her best friend."

His thumb caressed the back of her hand as he thought about everything she'd told him. Savannah hadn't just lost someone she'd loved. She'd gone through years of watching her friend struggle to live. Clearly, the experience was still affecting her deeply.

"That's tough, Savannah. Really tough."

A resigned smile curved her lips. "Yes. But everyone goes through rough spots in their life. My loss isn't any more or less important than the next person's."

He suddenly realized how much he wanted to gather her close to him and press his cheek against the top of her head. He wanted to hold her until she forgot about her friend. Until she forgot everything, but him.

But that sort of wishful craving would only get him into trouble. And not just the kind that caused a heartbreak. No, if Miles Fortune believed Chaz had touched his daughter in a romantic or sexual way, he'd fire him on the spot.

"Anyway, I just wanted you to know," she went on. "That's why—in the garden I was looking at the sculpture of cherubs and all of a sudden it reminded me of Bethann."

"Perhaps she was thinking about you."

She smiled at him and this time her eyes were shining. "That's a nice thought, Chaz. Very nice."

Something turned over in the middle of his chest and though he had enough strength to disengage his hand from hers, he couldn't find enough willpower to move away from her.

"You told me you were studying about diseases. Why

people get them and how to prevent them. This doctorate you're after—does it have anything to do with losing your friend?"

His question appeared to surprise her and then after a moment, she nodded. "Watching her try to fight the disease made me angry and helpless. I wanted to do something so badly. Once she was gone, I understood it was too late to do anything *for* her. But I could do something *because* of her. I think she'd be pleased to know I am trying to make a difference for other people. At least, I'm hoping that once I finish my education I'll be able to make a difference in the world of research."

When Chaz had met Savannah at the airport, he'd told himself he didn't want to know anything about her personal life. The less he knew about her, the easier it would be to let his job stand as a barrier between them. But now he was glad that she'd shared a part of her past with him. He was glad to learn that she was far more than a rich little princess playing at life.

"You will make a difference someday. And, Savannah, if I seemed brusque yesterday—it had nothing to do with your tears. Just forget it. Okay?"

"If you want me to."

"I do."

After he spoke, silence fell between them, but it was the companionable sort and as they sat there together in the darkness, Chaz couldn't remember ever feeling okay to simply sit with a woman. Saying nothing. Doing nothing. Except pleasantly absorbing the warmth of her thigh pressed against his and her sweet, sultry scent floating around her.

"During the eight years I was in the army, I saw plenty of bad sights," he remarked. "Once something like that gets in your head, it's impossible to get out."

For long moments, she quietly studied him. "Were you ever deployed?"

"Three times. First to Germany, the last two to the Middle East."

"That's serious. Did you lose any buddies?"

"I did. One by ambush. Two when the vehicle they were traveling in hit an IED." Strange, he thought, but during those structured years he'd spent in the army, he'd felt more free than at any other time in his life. Free of his family's scrutiny, free of the futileness of loving a woman who'd never really loved him in return.

Savannah shivered and Chaz wondered if she was the clingy sort, who'd be afraid to let her husband work a dangerous job. Would the worry and stress be too much for her to handle?

Hell, why was he wondering about that sort of thing? If by some far-off chance he decided he wanted to take a wife, it would hardly be a Fortune woman. Besides, for all he knew, Savannah might be dating a law officer back in New Orleans.

"I'm sure your family was relieved when you decided to return to civilian life," she remarked.

He shrugged. "They were glad I moved here to Austin and all of them are proud of my service to our country. If any of them worried about my safety, they didn't let on."

"What made you want to go into the army?" Her gaze turned curious. "Has anyone else in your family served in the military?"

"My Uncle Orlando was a pilot in the air force," he told her. "But I wasn't necessarily trying to follow in his footsteps. I first entered the ROTC as a way to get my college education."

Her brows arched with interest. "Oh. I'm rather ignorant about such things, but I thought members of the ROTC only did their military service state-side."

"Most do. But after I finished college, I decided to go full-time army."

He could feel her gaze probing his face, searching for answers he wasn't ready to give her. When he'd told her that Orlando's service in the air force hadn't influenced him to enter the army, he'd not been totally honest. Back then, he'd wanted to be more like his uncle and less like his father.

"That was admirable," she finally said.

Chaz couldn't remember any woman calling him admirable. But then he didn't talk about himself to any of the women he dated. Most women enjoyed talking about themselves and Chaz found it easier to just listen. That way he didn't have to reveal much about himself. He didn't have to risk the chance of an emotional connection developing. Yet, during these past few days, he was discovering that everything felt different when he was with Savannah. *She* was different.

"Don't get me wrong, Savannah. I wasn't necessarily trying to be noble. Serving in the army just felt like the best thing for me at that time."

She smiled at him again and Chaz felt the sincerity of her expression drawing him in and making him wonder whether she really might be different from Allison. Maybe all the wealth and privilege of being a Fortune hadn't separated her from regular folks like him.

"So what did you study in college?" she asked.

His short cynical laugh summed up his struggles in the classroom. "I wasn't like you. Learning was a real effort for me. After I scraped through the basics, I geared everything toward criminal justice."

"Mmm. That covers a wide spectrum. What plans did you have? I mean in the way of a job?"

"Law enforcement. That's why I was contemplating being an MP. But then the pull of my family changed my thinking and I decided to move here to Austin."

"Because you felt they needed you?"

He shrugged. "No. Because I needed them more."

"Oh."

Chaz was jealous of the moonlight kissing her face. He wished he had the right to slide his lips along her cheekbones, down her nose and onto the luscious curves of her mouth. He figured kissing her would be like dipping into a bowl of crushed berries sweetened with sugar.

Trying to shove away the forbidden urge, he asked, "Does that surprise you?"

"Actually, it does. You don't seem like a man who needs anyone but yourself."

Chaz had never thought of himself as an isolated man. A man who wanted to be totally independent of others. But apparently she viewed him in that manner and he wasn't at all sure he liked the image.

"Everybody needs someone, Savannah."

"But some don't want to admit they do," she said. "I've always had my parents and siblings around me. I wouldn't know what it was like to be entirely alone. I hope I never have to find out."

He gave her a droll smile. "You'll never have that problem, Savannah. I'm betting you probably have a list of boyfriends back in New Orleans just waiting on your return."

Her mouth fell open in a comical way and then she let out a soft laugh. "Excuse me, but would you repeat that so I can video it on my phone and send it to my sisters? They'd get a huge laugh."

As his gaze slipped over her, he couldn't help thinking Savannah was more than a mark for Charlotte Robinson's revenge. With her beauty and wealth, she had to be a huge target for men with self-gain on their minds. Maybe Chaz was stupid, but in spite of her travels and going through years of college, he was beginning to see she was still naive and vulnerable in many ways. To think of some greedy jerk taking advantage of her soft heart, some creep putting his hands on her, made his stomach churn.

"Why would your sisters laugh?" he asked.

Her gaze fell to her lap and though he couldn't see her face clearly, Chaz got the impression she was blushing.

Did women actually do that nowadays? Not the ones he dated, he thought ruefully. Modesty was something their grandmothers practiced, not them.

So what's the problem, Chaz? You're the one who chose to date them. All you want with a woman is fun and games anyway. And you sure won't get that with a woman that blushes.

Chaz was relieved when the jeering voice in his head was suddenly interrupted with her answer.

"Because my sisters call me the science spinster," she said glumly. "They're convinced I'll live the rest of my life with my career and nothing else."

Chaz had no business asking, but he did anyway. "Is that what you want for your future?"

She looked up and for a moment he thought he spotted a mist of moisture in her eyes.

"No! I mean—I don't want a man in my life right now. But that doesn't mean I always want to be single. Someday, after I finish my education and find my dream job, I'd like to have a husband, and children, and a home of my own."

"A home on Bourbon Street. With an inner court-yard and a balcony where you can hear the faint sound of someone playing the blues. And if you get the urge for beignets and coffee for breakfast, all you have to do is walk down the street to a little outdoor café. Right?"

The smile on her face was dreamy and he realized that pleasing this woman would certainly feed a man's ego. Hell, it would probably make him feel like he could bend a piece of steel with his bare hands or pluck a star from the sky.

"What's wrong with that?" she asked.

"Nothing. It all sounds nice. If you have the right man with you," he added slyly.

"I'll make sure he's the right man."

"By waiting until everything is perfect?"

His question put an annoyed look on her face. "I don't believe you have a wife and children tucked away any-where. What are you waiting for?"

"We weren't talking about me," he said bluntly.

"You brought up the subject. So you opened the door for cross-examination," she pointed out cleverly.

"You haven't been telling me the truth," he muttered. "You've been studying to be a trial lawyer. Not epide-miology."

She laughed softly. "When Miles Fortune is your fa-ther, you have to learn how to argue your case. And even then, he usually wins."

Yes, Chaz could very well imagine. He'd never met Savannah's father face-to-face, but during his phone calls with Miles, he'd detected the man's controlling attitude.

"I suppose this means you expect me to answer your question about a wife and children."

One of her slender shoulders lifted and fell. "Thoughts about love and marriage are private matters. And you've only known me a short time. I would understand if you tell me to mind my own business."

Only a short time. Why was it beginning to feel like he'd known her for much, much longer? How was it that everything about her was already burned into his memory?

He let out a heavy breath. "Okay, since you asked, I date whenever the mood hits me. But as far as me in a special relationship—that isn't going to happen."

She didn't make a reply. But then, she didn't need to. Confusion and disapproval were marching across her face.

He made a dismissive gesture with his hand. "Look, I don't have anything against marriage. As long as it's the other guy and not me. I'm not the type to settle down in a two-story house with a bunch of little Mendozas running around my feet. Besides, in my line of work, I need my independence."

"Hmm. I guess it would be rather awkward explaining to your wife that you had to leave for a few weeks or months to protect another woman. She might not approve."

Stints as a bodyguard didn't come along every day for Chaz. And once this one ended, he was going to make damned sure he was going back to his rule of not accepting a woman client.

"I figure she'd have to be a special person to approve of the job," he said drolly.

"It's too bad that you consider being a bodyguard more important to you than having a wife and children," she murmured.

He countered with a question. "Like you consider finding a job in epidemiology more important?"

A faint smile gradually curved the corners of her lips.

"Okay. I guess neither of us is interested in finding love and a spouse. But that hardly makes us abnormal. A person doesn't have to be a husband or wife to be a well-rounded human being."

Chaz didn't understand why he continued to sit here, tempting and torturing himself. Her luscious scent and soft lilting voice were lulling him into a false paradise. He needed to move to some other spot on the patio. He needed to forget about touching her. Kissing her.

Rising from the glider, he said, "I have some safety checks I need to make on my laptop. I'd better go in and get them done," he said gruffly.

She quickly stood and the movement caused her arm to brush against his. The contact was like having a branding iron sear his flesh and he immediately took a step back.

The reprieve was only momentary as she suddenly stunned him by moving forward and gently resting a hand upon his forearm.

"Chaz, I'm sorry. All my talking has made you uncomfortable and that wasn't my intention. But I'm glad that you listened. I'm glad that you told me a bit about yourself. Now it doesn't feel like we're two strangers living under the same roof."

"We should've remained strangers," he said, his voice hoarse from the need to pull her into his arms.

Her eyes widened just a fraction. "Really? Why?"

He groaned and then suddenly his fingertips were trailing down her cheek and along the edge of her jaw. Her skin was softer than velvet. Softer than anything he'd ever touched. His fingers longed to slip downward to where the tiny strap of her top rested on her shoulder. And farther still to the shadowy vee between her breasts.

"Because now that we know each other better, I want to do this. And this." Bending his head, he touched his lips to her temple, then to her forehead and down to the tip of her nose.

When his lips finally hovered over hers, she let out a soft sigh. Her breath brushed his face, while the needy sound pierced him in the middle of his chest like a burning arrow. His heart missed a beat and his lungs refused to work. If he didn't kiss her in the next five seconds, he figured he would surely die from longing.

"Chaz."

His name came out like the whisper of a breeze, while at the same time her fingers were fluttering against his chest, searching for a place to safely land.

"Don't tell me this is wrong," he murmured. "I already know it is."

Her lips parted, but she didn't utter a word. Chaz took advantage of her silence and closed the tiny chasm between their lips.

The contact was ethereal. Like touching a cloud and floating through a sky so bright and beautiful he had to close his eyes to be able to bear the wonder of it all.

This was not a kiss, he thought. This was an experience unlike anything he'd had before. It was sweet perfection and a connection he didn't want to end.

But the end did finally arrive when she stepped back and stared at him in complete dismay.

"What was that?" she whispered hoarsely.

His lips twisted to a rueful slant. "That was me being the biggest fool you've ever met."

Her chin quivered ever so slightly and Chaz had to fight with himself to keep from reaching out and dragging her into the circle of his arms.

"And what does that make me for kissing you back?" She wanted to know. "The second biggest fool?"

He shook his head. "This moment is over, Savannah. Gone. Never to be repeated. Understand?"

She licked her lips and Chaz inwardly groaned as desire suddenly gripped his loins.

"Not exactly," she answered.

"Then I'll explain it in plain, simple words. If I kiss you again, I'm going to have to take myself off the job. Your father will have to find someone else to be your bodyguard."

She looked crestfallen and Chaz wondered if her reaction had more to do with no more kisses or his leaving.

"Oh. Then we'd better stay away from each other. As far as possible."

"Yeah. As far as possible." Bending down, he picked up his dessert plate and coffee mug, then started toward the house. Midway to the patio doors, he looked over his shoulder at her. "I'm sorry this happened, Savannah."

Not bothering to collect her dirty dishes, she hurried over to where he stood. "Why? I'm not."

Chaz groaned with frustration. "Then you obviously don't care whether I lose this job. I thought—"

"You thought what?"

Like a fool, he'd been thinking she was beginning to like him as a person. That his feelings mattered.

"Nothing," he said stonily.

A frown wrinkled her features. "I don't understand you, Chaz. Whether you want to kiss me or I want to kiss you has nothing to do with my father. Please don't use him as an excuse to wedge a barrier between us."

Maybe she believed her father wasn't a wedge between them, but Chaz fully grasped the situation. Miles Fortune would never recognize him as worthy of his daughter's attentions, much less ever consider him as son-in-law material. And where Savannah was concerned, there was only one option with her. Marry her or leave her for someone else. She wasn't affair material. Not for Chaz, or any other man.

"Okay, I won't use your father as an excuse. I'll make it even clearer. You and I are from different worlds. Where you open a can of caviar, I rip the lid off a can of soup."

She smiled at him and for the first time in years, he felt an emotional lump building in his throat.

"You're very wrong about that, Chaz. But I'm not going to waste my time trying to change your mind tonight. Soon you'll see it for yourself."

He was still contemplating her words, when she rose on the tips of her toes and planted a soft kiss to the side of his face.

"And by the way, you can't count that little kiss," she said with an impish grin. "Good night, Chaz."

Turning away from him, she collected her dirty dishes, then went into the house. As Chaz watched her disappear through the patio doors, he could see an explosion on the horizon and he figured that once the dust settled, the only thing left of him would be a few broken pieces.

Chapter Eight

"Are you feeling okay, Savannah?"

Savannah glanced across the break room table to where Marva was sitting in a chair next to Arnold, one of the male members of the study group. At twenty-six, he needed several more hours of studies to get his postgraduate degree, but on the subject of diseases, he was light-years beyond Savannah. Quiet, with an odd penchant for dressing like Elvis, he'd instinctively gravitated toward Savannah and Marva, rather than some of the other men in the group. Savannah appreciated his brainpower and his humbleness.

Savannah answered while thinking she should have added more concealer to the dark circles under her eyes.

"I'm fine, Marva. Why? Do I look sick?"

"Not exactly. More like preoccupied."

With one little kiss, Savannah thought. No, it hadn't been little, she corrected herself. It had been gigantic! Monumental! It had changed every plan she'd ever made.

Every hope and dream she'd ever carried around in her heart.

Clearing her throat, she reached for the foam cup of coffee she was having with her lunch.

She said, "This study group is much more difficult than I imagined."

"That's an understatement," Arnold muttered, then leaning his head toward to the two women, he lowered his voice. "Honestly, it's hell trying to follow Professor Barcroft's lectures. He drifts and drifts until he's so far-off course I get to thinking I'm somewhere in left field watching for fly balls."

"Same here," Marva added with a grimace. "And I thought he was supposed to be one of the best."

"Well, this is only our second day," Savannah reasoned. "I'm guessing we need more time to get used to his style of teaching."

"Don't you mean get used to his arrogance?" Marva asked, with a shake of her head. "God forgive me, but he reminds me of my ex-brother-in-law. My sister divorced him because she couldn't stand his conceit. Too bad I can't divorce this professor."

Arnold glanced at the older woman. "It's not a requirement that you stay, Marva."

"I'm not about to leave," she said resolutely. "Since the study group has already started, I doubt they'd allow anyone to fill my vacancy. Besides, I'm not a quitter. This is too important for me."

"Same here," Savannah said. "My being here has already caused a rift between me and my father. I need to prove to him that this study group was the right thing for me to do."

Arnold glanced at her. "Where are you from originally, Savannah?"

She looked across the table, while wondering why a man like him couldn't catch her attention. Arnold wasn't a hard hunk of muscle like Chaz, nor did he have his dark good looks. But he was slender and fit, and his smiles were the kind that assured her it would be a freezing July day before he'd raise his voice in anger to anyone. As for the subject of science, he was highly intelligent and devoted to his studies. He might not be exciting or sexy, but he'd make some woman a nice husband. At least, he'd be a damned sight gentler to the heart than a playboy like Chaz.

I'm not the type to settle down in a two-story house with a bunch of little Mendozas running around my feet.

Chaz's remark shouldn't be bothering her. Whether he wanted to play the field for the rest of his life or have a wife and eight children was really nothing to her. Like she'd told him, she wasn't looking for a man. It would be years before she started thinking about marriage and babies. And yet, hearing him say he wasn't interested in love was like hearing a person didn't like flowers, or birds, or ice cream. It just wasn't natural.

Shaking herself out of her glum reverie, she answered Arnold's question. "I live in the Garden District in New Orleans."

He nodded slightly. "I've been there. I live in New Mexico. Santa Fe. We still had snow on the mountains when I left home."

"And it already feels like summer here," Marva replied with a chuckle. "Hope you brought your shorts and sunscreen."

He frowned. "At the rate I'm going, I doubt I'll have a chance to spend any time outdoors. I'll be too busy trying to unravel the professor's lectures."

The three of them discussed their studies a few more

minutes before Arnold excused himself from the utility table. Once he was gone, Savannah began to gather her leftovers and pack them back into an insulated lunch sack.

"Ten minutes until lab class," Marva said, as she checked her watch. "At least we'll get to look at microscope slides or do some sort of chemical tests rather than take notes."

"It would be a refreshing change," Savannah agreed, then looked thoughtfully over at the woman. "Marva, you told me that your children are grown. Do you have a daughter?"

"One. Kathy is married with two youngsters. A boy and a girl. She's the first one of my children to make me a grandmother."

Savannah smiled. "If she takes after her mother at all, I'm sure I'd like her. I was asking because—"

"Because you need to talk with me about something?"

Relieved, Savannah nodded. "Oh, Marva, from the moment I arrived in Austin nothing has been like I expected."

"And you're homesick?"

She shook her head. "No. I guess you could say I'm a little scared."

Marva's attitude changed to one of concern. "Scared. To live alone in your apartment? Has someone been threatening you?"

Savannah sounded like a child who was too immature to take care of herself. "No one has directly threatened me. And I'm not living alone while I'm in Austin. My father has hired a bodyguard to protect me around the clock. As far as I know, my bodyguard could be staked out on campus right now. Watching to make sure no suspicious looking characters enter or exit the building."

Marva's mouth dropped open. "Dear Lord, I've always wanted my children to be safe, but I never reached the point of hiring a bodyguard! I couldn't have afforded one anyway."

Savannah had never been one to talk about her personal life with fellow students or even with friends. Not that she had that many close friends. After Bethann had died, she'd made a point to avoid getting that close to anyone again. But Marva had a maternal warmth about her and Savannah needed to share her troubled thoughts with someone.

"This isn't something I go around telling and please don't let it affect our friendship, Marva. You see, my family is wealthy. Extremely wealthy. My father owns Fortune Investments in New Orleans."

Marva's amazement quickly changed to understanding. "Oh, I see. He worries about kidnappers."

Kidnappers? Not exactly, Savannah thought. No one had implied to Savannah that the threat against the Fortunes involved money. But she supposed the possibility couldn't be ruled out. And it was easier to let Marva think along those lines, rather than making an attempt to explain Gerald Robinson's connection to the family and that his ex-wife was supposedly plotting revenge.

"Something like that," Savannah told her.

The woman shook her head. "Well, rest assured I'm not going to let anything ruin our new friendship, Savannah. Besides, I don't have anything against rich people."

Savannah's laugh was a short dry burst of sound. "I'm glad. Not everyone feels like you." She sucked in a long bracing breath. "But this matter of the bodyguard—I didn't know about him until I got here to Austin. My father didn't tell me. So meeting Chaz was a shock."

"Chaz? That's the bodyguard?"

Savannah nodded, then felt her cheeks begin to burn red as the memory of his kiss washed over her. She'd been kissed before, but none of those occasions could begin to match the experience of having Chaz's lips on hers. She'd felt euphoric, and exposed and everything in between. How was she supposed to concentrate when all she could think about was kissing him again?

"Yes. And he's—uh, very handsome and strong and difficult to ignore. I'm afraid I'm beginning to like him far too much."

"I'm getting the picture. Is he single?"

Savannah nodded. "And from what he says, he's determined to remain that way."

Marva made a dismissive gesture with her hand. "They all say that. Most men are just waiting to be caught."

If possible, the heat in Savannah's cheeks grew even hotter. "Chaz isn't the type to stand still and let a woman snare him. Besides, I don't want to catch him. I want to get him off my mind." She gave her head a helpless shake. "The whole thing sounds silly, doesn't it?"

"No. It sounds perfectly normal to me. A pretty girl like you housed up with a handsome hunk. You'd be dead not to feel some sparks."

She'd felt sparks all right. More like fireworks.

"I don't want to have my thoughts distracted from this study group, Marva. I have so many plans for a job, a career. I want my education to mean something important."

Marva reached across the table and patted Savannah's hand. "Honey, you're worrying too much. Being attracted to a handsome man is hardly a crime or the end of the world. Even if he is your bodyguard."

Savannah gave her a wobbly smile. "Put like that I guess I sound like my father. And God knows I don't want to be as autocratic or controlling as him."

"Maybe you should talk to your mother about this," she suggested.

Savannah shook her head. "Mother is very supportive and I will be talking with her, but I won't mention any of this to her."

"Why not? Mothers are good about listening and advising."

Grimacing, she explained, "Because as soon as she got off the phone she'd repeat everything I said to Dad. She loves her children, but she's one of those wives who believes her husband should know *everything*. And that would cause all kinds of problems. Dad would probably fly up here and collect me himself."

Marva frowned. "Just how old are you, Savannah?"

Another blush warmed her cheeks. "Twenty-five."

"That's a grown woman. By the time I was your age, I was married and had two kids. Maybe you should remind your father that you're on a college campus, not an elementary school playground."

"That might be easier said than done," Savannah told her. "There are seven of us children and he tries to direct each one of our lives. His daughters more so than his sons."

Marva gave her another understanding smile. "That's because he loves you."

If I kiss you again, I'm going to have to take myself off the job.

Would Chaz really do that? How would she feel if he did?

Lost. Empty. That's how she would feel.

The troubling thoughts continued to nag her as Marva rose to her feet and collected the trash left over from her lunch.

"We'd better head to the lab," she said. "I've already learned one thing. Professor Barcroft is very prompt."

Savannah had learned something, too, she thought, as she followed Marva out of the break room. If she weren't careful, she was going to fall head over heels for Chaz Mendoza. A man who would never return her feelings.

Three days later at the family distribution center in Austin Commons, Chaz watched his brother Carlo shove a box of wine onto the stack the two men had created at the back of the storage room.

"That's the last of the merlot," Carlo announced. "A steak house across town has been selling the heck out of this stuff."

"Do we have more at the winery?"

"Unfortunately, no. After this goes, we'll be sold out. Which, on one hand, is a good thing. On the flip side, it's going to hurt when we have to tell our customers there won't be any for a long while." He thoughtfully studied the stack of boxes. "We need to plant more black grapes for the merlot. That much is obvious."

"Even if Alejandro can find the extra ground, it will take a few years to get the vines up and producing," Chaz pointed out.

"Good wine isn't made in a day, my brother," Carlo said cheerfully. "But it can sure make a day good."

Chaz snorted. Carlo would look at the bright side of things. He'd found his rainbow riches when he'd married Schuyler Fortunado. The beautiful blonde had made his brother happier than he'd ever seen him. Not only that, she'd changed a dedicated playboy into a contented, one-woman man. It was still hard for Chaz to believe.

"A little wine will fix everything, huh? Well, I'm glad I'm only the security man."

Carlo turned a scowl on him. "Only? What does that mean? Handling the security for the Mendoza businesses is a big deal. And it's going to become an even bigger deal for you once we add the wine bar and the nightclub."

Chaz shrugged, while hating himself for sounding so crabby. Carlo hadn't done anything to him. Except show him everything that was missing in his life. Like a woman who truly loved him.

"If you say so."

Carlo walked over and stood facing him. "What's the matter with you? Have you argued with Dad about something?"

"No. I've not even seen Dad or talked with him since last Sunday when Savannah and I visited the winery. And there's nothing wrong with me that a good night's sleep won't fix."

Carlo darted him a sly glance. "What's the problem? Your pretty Miss Fortune is a loud snorer and she's keeping you awake at night?"

Chaz's fingers unconsciously curled into loose fists. Any other time, his brother's teasing would have rolled off his back. But not this time. Not when Savannah was the subject. "Since I'm sleeping in a bedroom across from her, I couldn't say whether she snores loudly, or at all. Last night, an alarm went off at the winery and I was up several hours trying to detect what had set it off."

"Why didn't you or the security guard call me? Was anything amiss?"

"Nothing missing. Nothing vandalized. But I'll be honest, for a while I was wondering if Charlotte had sent her goons out to the winery to cause some mischief."

Chaz's suggestion clearly stunned his brother.

"Surely not! Why would she want to cause the Mendozas any problems?"

"I don't have any proof that she does. But think about it, Carlo. The Mendozas are tightly intertwined with the

Fortune family. Several Mendozas are married to Fortunes, including you. To hurt us would be hurting the Fortunes, too."

"Hmm. I never thought about it that way. But then my mind doesn't work like yours, Chaz. Danger, security risks, safety issues, you pick up on those things instantly. They have to be pointed out to me."

"Yes, but I don't have your business mind," Chaz retorted. "Like how many bottles of merlot we might sell in one day or one week. Or what kind of prices are needed on La Viña's dinner specials in order for the restaurant to make a profit."

"That's exactly right, brother. We each bring something different to Mendoza businesses and it takes all of us to make them work efficiently." Grinning, Carlo slung an affectionate arm around Chaz's shoulder and urged him out of the storage room. "Come on. Let's go to the main office and see if we can find something cold to drink."

"I'm all for that."

Down a long hallway, the two brothers entered a small office where the arrival and departure of inventory was logged in to a computer. Along with a desk and executive chair, the room also held a navy blue couch, three tall file cabinets, a compact refrigerator, a serving cart loaded with a coffee machine and all the fixings to go with it.

Chaz went straight to the refrigerator and peered inside. "Looks like we can choose from diet soda, green tea or water. Damn, what happened to all the beer? A few days ago, there were two six packs in here."

Carlo chuckled. "I asked Schuyler to restock the refrigerator and she's currently on a health kick. I'm guessing she moved the beer to make room for something with less calories. Looks as though there aren't any boxes of pastries over here with the coffee, either."

"What's next? Celery sticks and bean sprouts for snacks?" Chaz muttered as he pulled two cans of colas from the fridge and handed one of them to his brother.

"Just think of all the good it's doing your waistline." Carlo gestured to the couch. "Let's sit. We can waste a few minutes before we head out to the winery for another load."

Chaz eased into a cushion on one end of the couch and crossed his ankles out in front of him. Carlo joined him on the opposite end and quickly popped the top on his soda can. Chaz did the same and chugged down a third of the can in one gulp.

Carlo asked, "Have you told Alejandro about the incident with the security alarm?"

"Not yet. I want to check out a few more things before I give him a report."

Carlo's expression took a serious turn. "Were you really serious when you talked about Charlotte Robinson possibly making mayhem for us Mendozas?"

"Damn right. A mother who would cause her own son to get gravely injured will stop at nothing to get back at the Fortunes. Even if she has to go through the Mendozas to do it. And I wouldn't put it past her to bribe a worker in the winery or restaurant to spy for her. She could gather lots of information about us and the Fortunes that way."

Groaning, Carlo wiped a hand over his face. "That's a frightening idea. But how the hell would we know if anyone was secretly working for Charlotte? I'm telling you, Chaz, it scares the hell out of me to allow Schuyler to travel around the city on her own. Some of Charlotte's goons could be tailing her and… Well, I don't have to tell you what it would do to me if something happened to my wife. She's—"

"She's everything to you," Chaz finished for his brother. "Your life."

Carlo nodded, then slanted Chaz an unabashed grin. "It still amazes me that I can love someone as much as I love Schuyler. I didn't think I had it in me."

"I didn't think you had it in you, either," Chaz said in a deadpan voice.

Carlo was still laughing when a light knock had both men glancing toward the open doorway.

"Am I interrupting?"

Chaz watched his brother's face light up with joy as Schuyler stepped into the office.

"Speak of an angel and she appears." Carlo rose from the couch and greeted his wife with a kiss to her cheek.

The blonde beauty directed an impish smile at both men. "Have you two been talking about me?"

"Only good things, sweetheart." Carlo curled an arm around her waist. "What are you doing here anyway?"

"I had a few errands to run before the tasting party this afternoon. I wanted to go over a few things with you before the event, so I stopped by on the chance I might catch you here. Lucky for me, I did."

The provocative look she gave her husband made Chaz feel like a third wheel. It also made him wonder how it would feel to have a woman like Savannah look at him with that kind of genuine love.

Damn it, Chaz. You're not supposed to be thinking about Savannah.

Chaz mentally cursed at the images in his head. Savannah had ruined any chance of him ever having an enjoyable date. How could he find pleasure in another woman's company while his mind was saturated with thoughts of Savannah? With the need of kissing her again, removing every stitch of her expensive clothing and making hot, urgent love to her?

Chaz purposely turned his attention to his sister-in-law. "There is such a thing as a phone, Schuyler."

Laughing at his suggestion, she moved away from her husband and took a seat next to Chaz.

"One of these days, Chaz, you're going to learn what it's like to be married. Then you'll understand that a phone conversation just isn't the same as the real thing."

"Don't waste your time on him, honey," Carlo warned with a hint of sarcasm. "He's too busy hanging on to the past to ever let himself be happy."

Schuyler darted her husband a perplexed look before she turned a smile back on Chaz.

"Actually, I'm even more pleased that I've bumped into you, Chaz."

Her expression was more calculating than thoughtful and Chaz braced himself. He'd already learned his sister-in-law was the adventurous sort. Once she made a plan, she refused to let anyone or anything stand in the way.

"What's wrong?" Chaz asked. "Are you already getting tired of Carlo's ugly mug?"

"Not a chance." She winked at her husband, then turned back to Chaz. "I've been planning on calling Savannah, but doing this through you might be better. Since she doesn't really know me that well—yet."

"This," he repeated warily. "What is *this*?"

Schuyler answered cheerfully, "For the four of us to have dinner together at La Viña. Savannah is one of my new cousins. I'd love to have the chance to spend a bit of time with her. Can you arrange it with her? Perhaps tomorrow night? At seven?"

Chaz tried not to flinch. He already had hours of being

with Savannah in a family setting. Hours he was going to have to work at forgetting. He didn't need to add to the problem.

"Why dinner at La Viña?" he asked, careful to keep any irritation from his voice. "I'm sure she'd be fine with you visiting the apartment. You two can talk all you want."

Schuyler scowled at him. "That's not the same. I want the four of us to be together—as a family. I'm hoping it will, at least, make her feel more wanted by the Fortunado branch of the family. Now that I think about it, let's make the time six. That way we can have wine and hors d'oeuvres and a leisurely talk before dinner."

"I think that's a great idea, Schuyler," Carlo said, while over his wife's head, he leveled a pointed look at Chaz. One that warned him not to try to weasel out of this. "I'm glad you thought of it."

The four of us...together—as a family. What was Schuyler thinking? Savannah was just a woman he was protecting. She wasn't *his* family. But protesting too loudly would only rouse suspicions and the last thing he needed was for Carlo and Schuyler to get the notion that Chaz was falling for Savannah. If word like that ever got out, it would be the end of his career as a bodyguard.

Hell, who are you kidding, Chaz? You're not worried about your career. You're more concerned about having your heart torn right out of your chest.

Disgusted with the voice plowing through his head, he purposely plastered a smile on his face. "I'll ask Savannah this evening and let you know what she thinks," he said.

Schuyler gave him a bright smile. "Great! Thank you, Chaz! You're the best brother-in-law a girl could have."

The remark drew a chuckle from Carlo. "She tells Mark, Rodrigo, Stefan and Joaquin all the same thing."

"I do not!" Schuyler exclaimed, then poked a playful finger in her husband's ribs. "Now. About this afternoon. I was thinking—"

While Carlo discussed the wine tasting party with his wife, Chaz walked over to the one window in the office. Beyond the glass there was little more to see than a paved alleyway where box trucks parked to unload their freight. But the dreary view didn't register with Chaz. Instead, he was only seeing a blue spring sky, an occasional wisp of a cloud floating overhead and Savannah's lovely face.

Chapter Nine

Later that afternoon, Professor Barcroft surprised the whole study group by ending the last class a few minutes early.

After telling Marva and Arnold a quick goodbye, Savannah carried her tote bag out to the park bench where Chaz normally waited for her. He was nowhere in sight, so she decided to take a seat on the bench and use the opportunity to call her sister while she waited for him to arrive.

As director of public relations for Fortune Investments in New Orleans, Georgia was always overloaded with work and stretched for time. But Savannah was hoping her sister might have a moment or two to share with her. Since Georgia was three years older, she'd always looked up to her for advice and guidance. Two things that Savannah could certainly use right about now.

Georgia answered the call with a scolding question.

"What in the heck have you been doing, sis? I'd practically given up on you calling!"

Chuckling, Savannah asked, "Uh, are you going to give me a chance to say hello?"

"Okay, tell me hello and then tell me everything that's been happening. You know, Mom is getting really peeved at you. Those few short texts you've sent her is not enough to convince her that you're well and happy."

Savannah held back a long sigh. "I haven't exactly gotten any calls from you or Mom, either," she pointed out to her sister.

"Sorry. We've both been very busy. And I convinced Mom that we needed to give you time to get settled before we pestered you with phone calls."

Smiling, Savannah said, "Thanks, sis. I am well and happy. And in case you've all forgotten, I have an overload of work going on up here. Actually, more than I expected. Our professor is a taskmaster."

"Forget about your damned professor! I want to hear about the bodyguard! *Your* bodyguard! Belle is dying to see a picture of him. Can you message her one?"

"No! I don't even have a picture of Chaz! And I wouldn't send it to Belle anyway. What does she think this is, fun and games?"

"Well, she and I both know it's not fun and games with you, but it might be to us. Seeing that we view men in a slightly different light than you."

From the suggestive drawl in Georgia's voice, it was obvious that her office was empty for the moment.

Savannah rolled her eyes skyward. "Right now, I'm asking myself why I even bothered to call. To get insulted, I suppose."

Georgia let out a good-natured groan. "Oh, sissy, I'm only kidding. We've been missing you like crazy down here. What's it like in Austin? Are the people really as weird as they say?"

Smiling, Savannah shook her head. "I can't honestly give you a fair assessment on whether Austin folks are weird. I've not met that many people yet and the ones I have met are not Austin natives. I'm stuck on campus every day of the week. And Chaz doesn't want me to go out and about by myself."

"Chaz," Georgia repeated thoughtfully. "Mom told us his last name is Mendoza. Is he related to that good-looking Mendoza guy that Schuyler Fortunado married?"

"They're brothers. And before you ask, yes, Chaz is just as good-looking as Carlo. Only in a different way. He's built like a powerhouse. With short black hair that waves just enough to keep it from being straight and brown eyes that have lashes to die for. He also has a black mustache and goatee. The kind that's neat and trimmed."

The kind that made her fingers itch to stroke it, Savannah thought guiltily. And the kind of lips that made her knees too weak to bear the weight of a feather.

"Oooh, Savannah, what in the world has come over you? I've never heard you describe a man in those terms. I'm starting to think I should find a reason to fly up to Austin just to see for myself."

Closing her eyes, Savannah wearily pinched the bridge of her nose. Even though Georgia was teasing, she would know exactly how to handle herself around Chaz. Being in public relations, she dealt with all kinds of men. And Georgia's upbeat personality would probably be more to Chaz's liking than Savannah's serious disposition. The only men who liked women scientists were in the field of science themselves. She figured men like Chaz wanted a girlie girl, who was not only feminine and pretty but fun to be around. Not a bookworm like her who knew all about the causes of the plague, but was lost when it came to seducing a man.

"I wish you would fly up. It would be nice to see a familiar face right about now," Savannah said, more glumly than she'd intended.

There was a long pause before Georgia replied, "Why, sis, you sound very down in the dumps. What's going on? You were so excited about this study group. Other than the professor being a taskmaster, isn't it going well?"

Savannah turned her head away from the phone so her sister couldn't hear her troubled sigh. "The study group is great. I'm learning and making a few friends in the process. It's just that I—seriously, Georgia, having a bodyguard can be quite taxing on the nerves. And it makes things worse because he won't allow me to go out and about the city alone. I can't really do anything unless he deems it safe."

"Oh, that is a bummer," Georgia agreed. "But look at it this way, sis. What if you really were in danger and no one was around to help you?"

And what if you were falling helplessly for a man who considered marriage a communicable disease? Although she wanted to ask her sister the question, she held it back.

"You're right. And while I'm here, I'll deal with Chaz. For Dad's sake."

"For all our sakes," Georgia reminded her. "We all want you to be safe. God only knows what that wicked woman has on her mind next! I get so spooked just thinking about it that each time I leave the house, I find myself looking over my shoulder."

Savannah sat up straight on the edge of the bench. "Why are you getting spooked? Has Dad gotten more news about Charlotte?"

"I think he talked briefly yesterday with Connor Fortunado. I don't know exactly what was said, but he and Dad seem to think the woman has gone beyond revenge now. They think she's truly become unhinged. Which is understandable, I suppose. What woman wouldn't go half-crazy if her ex-husband had a list of lovers a mile long and plenty of illegitimate children to prove it?"

"True," Savannah glumly agreed. "Especially when the scandalous information is plastered all over the tabloids. But does that really have anything to do with our family? With me? I just can't see the motive."

"Do crazy people usually have reasonable motives for the things they do?"

"You got me there," Savannah mumbled, then forcing a more cheerful note to her voice, asked, "So what has been going on with the rest of the family? And have you bumped into Mr. Right yet?"

Georgia laughed. "I've not had time to take a deep breath. After getting a massive quarterly earnings report, Dad has hired ten new employees this past week. And he's asked me to develop a new media blitz to help pull in more accounts. I'm trying to put something innovative together for that."

"Just like he needs more accounts," Savannah said dryly.

Georgia was passing some of her advertising ideas by Savannah, when she suddenly spotted Chaz's black car brake to a jarring halt in the parking lot.

Once he departed the car, he closed the door with a bang and strode quickly up the sidewalk to where she was sitting. Even from a distance, Savannah could see he was fuming about something.

"Sorry to interrupt, sis. But I have to go. I'll call you later."

By the time Chaz reached the park bench where she

was sitting, Savannah had ended the connection. After slipping the cell phone back into her purse, she looked up to see he was standing over her, his face taut, his eyes snapping fire. He was someone she'd never seen before.

"What the hell do you think you're doing?"

He blasted the question at her and for a moment, Savannah stared at him in stunned silence.

"I beg your pardon?" she said when she finally managed to speak.

Mouthing a curse word under his breath, he wrapped a hand around her arm and tugged her off the bench.

"Let's go," he ordered. "Now!"

The domineering sound of his voice shocked her senses back into action and she promptly yanked her arm away from him and planted her feet on the sidewalk.

"Don't order me around like I'm a child!"

If possible, his jaw clamped even tighter. "If you don't want to be treated like a child, then start acting like an adult—if you're capable."

Furious now, she jerked the strap of her tote bag onto her shoulder and glared at him. "I don't know what your problem is, but—"

"My problem is you!" he practically shouted. "You not having an ounce of common sense!"

Her teeth snapped together as she brushed past him and stomped her way down the sidewalk toward the parking lot.

She didn't have to look to see if he was following. She could feel his ominous presence bearing down on her like a storm cloud about to unleash its fury. But at the moment, she didn't care if he was snorting flames from his nostrils. She was sick of him giving her orders. Sick of him trying to keep her confined. And more than sick of trying to hide her desire to be in his arms.

As soon as she reached the car, she tried the door handle and was relieved to find it unlocked. Not waiting for Chaz, she tossed her tote in the back floorboard, then climbed in and fastened her seat belt.

When he slid into the driver's seat and started the engine, she was staring straight ahead, her chin high. It wasn't until he was gunning the vehicle out of the parking lot that it dawned on Savannah that he was correct about her. She wasn't using common sense. Otherwise, she would've used her cell to call a taxi and told him to get the hell out of her life.

"Would you mind telling me what you thought you were doing?" he asked sharply.

Her gaze fixed on the street, she asked in a saccharine sweet voice, "At what point? What are you talking about?"

"Damn it!" he growled. "You *know* what I'm talking about!"

"I'm afraid I don't. But I'm sure you won't mind pointing out my mistakes. Especially since you never make any."

For the next three blocks, a heavy silence permeated the interior of the car. Savannah stared out the passenger window and wished with everything inside her that she was no different than the women going in and out of the stores and businesses lining the street, that she had the freedom to simply be Savannah. Not Savannah Fortune, a millionaire's daughter with a target on her back and a thorn in her heart.

"Did it never occur to you, even once, that you were sitting out in the wide open? That anyone could have come along and snatched you up? Taken a shot at you? Harmed you in some way?"

All of this over her sitting on a park bench? She wanted to smack him right in the mouth. And not with her lips!

Glaring at him, she said, "If the situation has become so bad that I can't sit on a bench outside my classroom, then I might as well give up and go hide in a cave. That isn't living, Chaz."

His tanned complexion turned a furious red. "Many more stunts like that and you won't be living! Literally!"

The idea of jumping out of the car at the next red light dashed through Savannah's mind, but just as quickly, she realized that would only give her a momentary escape from this man. He'd come after her. Or call the police. Then her father would be livid.

"Poor Chaz!" she said, her voice thick with sarcasm. "That would put you out of a job. Literally!"

His attention left the road long enough to shoot a glower in her direction. "For two cents, I'd call your father and tell him I'm finished with—"

His words broke off, but Savannah didn't need further explanation.

"Being my jailer?" she asked bitterly. Bending forward, she grabbed her handbag and, after a quick search through her wallet, tossed two pennies at him. The coins struck his thigh, then fell onto the seat near his crotch. "There. Your miseries of dealing with me are over!"

The remainder of the trip to her apartment was finished in charged silence. Once Chaz parked behind her rental car, a vehicle she had only driven once, Savannah hurried inside and shut herself in her bedroom.

Moments later, as she was changing out of the mint-green dress she'd worn to class, she heard Chaz entering the apartment and then his footsteps echoed down the short hallway leading to the bedrooms. For a few seconds, she held her breath, fearing he was going to knock on her door and tell her he was leaving.

No. He wouldn't leave just like that, she decided miserably. He was too much of a professional to walk away and leave her unprotected.

After a moment, the sound of footsteps continued on past her door, confirming her beliefs, and she sank weakly onto the side of the bed and dropped her face in her hands.

Chaz placed the lid back on the pot of spaghetti and glanced at the clock hanging on the wall behind the kitchen table. Two and a half hours had passed since Savannah had stomped into the apartment and disappeared behind the door of her bedroom.

Since that time, Chaz had tried to come to terms with his burst of temper and Savannah's reaction to it. Now that his anger had cooled, he could understand her outrage. He must have come across to her as a crazy man.

One thing was for certain, he'd learned little Miss Fortune was not a meek pushover when she was riled. Moreover, she seemed not to care one whit whether he walked away from the task of being her bodyguard.

The reality of that had not only surprised him, it had stung him hard. Which was a stupid reaction on his part. How could he have allowed himself to forget, even for a second, that Savannah was on the same social level as Allison? Women of their wealth and standing didn't suffer a broken heart over any man—they simply moved on.

Wearily, he wiped a hand over his face, then walked out of the kitchen and straight to Savannah's bedroom door.

After a light rap of his knuckles, he waited for what seemed like ages before she finally called out.

"Come in. The door isn't locked."

He didn't want to go into her bedroom. Hell, it was hard enough to keep his hands off her in the most public of places. Being in the bedroom with her was nearly as provocative as standing next to her without any clothes on.

Drawing in a bracing breath, he opened the door and stood just over the threshold. Across the room, Savannah was sitting in an armchair near the window. Beyond the glass panes, the red-gold rays from the setting sun surrounded her dark hair like a glowing halo. Just looking at her lovely image was enough to steal his breath.

Closing the hardbound book in her lap, she asked crisply, "Did you want something?"

I want you.

The thought was a reality Chaz could no longer avoid or deny. Yet, he didn't know what, if anything, he could do about it. He was Savannah's protector. It would go against all the rules to start a relationship with her. Yet, to be with her and not touch her was an agony that was growing worse with each passing day. To do the honorable thing would be to take himself off the case and out of the picture totally.

With that dire notion in mind, he moved deeper into the room until he was standing a short space from her chair.

"Yes, I do want something." He strained to get the words past his tight throat. "I want to...apologize."

She looked even more stunned than she had back on campus when he'd pulled her off the park bench.

"Apologize. Are you joking?" she asked, then shook her head ever so slightly. "No. I should know better than that. You're not much of a jokester."

"I've heard that women are drawn to men who can make them laugh. Unfortunately, I never had the knack for it."

The hardness in her hazel eyes softened slightly and Chaz felt his heart thud with hope. Long ago, he'd quit caring what any woman thought about him. Until Savannah had come along. Now, her forgiveness meant everything.

"What do you want to apologize for? Being an ass in general? Or for giving up on being my bodyguard?"

He reached into the front pocket of his blue jeans and pulled out the two cents she'd thrown at him.

"Here's your money," he said, handing her the copper coins.

As her fingers curled around the pennies, her gaze landed on his face. Chaz could hardly bear the pain and confusion he saw in her eyes.

"You're not quitting?"

"When I start a job, I do my best to finish it," he said flatly.

"I thought that you wanted out."

Her voice was soft now and it caused something in his chest to twist into a knot so tight he could scarcely breathe.

"You thought wrong."

"Oh."

He heaved out a breath in the hope it would force his lungs to begin working again.

"As for me being an ass in general, you're right." His voice sounded like he was coming down with the flu or had just sobered up from a three-day drunk. Pleading guilty had never been easy for Chaz. "I behaved like a first-class jerk. And I'm sorry. But when I saw you sitting there in the wide open, I was so damned scared I couldn't see straight. I shouldn't have lashed out at you and I hope you'll forgive me."

Her face was all tender compassion as she rose and stood before him.

"I accept your apology. And I apologize for causing you so much distress. The professor released us early," she explained. "You hadn't arrived yet, so I sat down and called my sister in New Orleans."

Closing his eyes, he passed a hand over his forehead. "That's perfectly normal behavior, Savannah. For anyone else. Just not for a member of the Fortune family. At least, not with everything that's been going on."

He opened his eyes just as she was turning her back to him.

"I hate this," she said. "I hate being a Fortune and everything that goes with it."

Her voice was choked with anguish and the sound put a strangle hold on his heart. Before he could stop himself, he folded his hands around her upper arms and drew her backward until her back was pressed to his chest and his cheek was nestled against her soft hair.

"And I hate that this is happening to you, Savannah. But everything will get better—eventually. Until then, I promise I won't let anything happen to you." To get to her, Charlotte or her hired thugs would have to go over his dead body, he thought fiercely.

Slowly she turned to face him and Chaz winced at the tears glazing her eyes.

"I shouldn't have gotten so angry with you, Chaz. I don't want you to leave. Not really."

In spite of everything, her words brought him a measure of joy, making it impossible to hold back a smile.

"I'm glad we got that out of the way."

"So am I."

"I've cooked a pot of spaghetti," he told her. "It's going to get cold if we don't go eat it."

Pleasant surprise chased away the shadows in her eyes. "You know how to cook spaghetti, too?"

He chuckled. "Besides acting like a jackass, I know how to do a few other things."

A tender smile touched her lips. "I am hungry. And spaghetti sounds wonderful."

With a hand against the small of her back, he urged her out of the bedroom. "Let's go eat."

At the kitchen table several minutes later, Savannah was halfway through the food on her plate when Chaz once again caught her by surprise.

"I have an invitation for you."

She paused in the act of twirling spaghetti around the tines of her fork and looked up at him.

"I'm guessing the invitation is from Dad—to return to New Orleans. Right?"

"No. Although, I'm sure you'd make your father a happy man if you did leave Austin."

She grimaced. "Georgia tells me that Dad and Connor Fortunado believe Charlotte has gone off the deep end. Have you heard any news about the woman?"

He shook his head. "Nothing concrete. I don't believe anyone has been able to pinpoint exactly where she's hidden herself away. Most likely, she's moving around to cover her tracks. But you can be sure she's not had a change of heart and decided to be a nice human being."

Savannah reached for her iced tea. "If it's not Dad, then what is this invitation?"

"My brother and sister-in-law would like for the two of us to join them for dinner tomorrow night at La Viña. Schuyler is all excited about seeing you again and she thought you'd be more open to the idea if I invited you." His lips took on a wry slant. "She doesn't know that you and I spend half our time squaring off with each other."

Savannah's gaze slid discreetly over his rugged face and broad shoulders. How could she be so furious with him one minute and desperately want to kiss him the next? She must be developing some sort of mental disease that she'd not yet studied, she decided.

"I wouldn't say half the time," she said with wry amusement. "More like an eighth or a tenth."

He chuckled and she tried to imagine how it might be if the two of them had met under different circumstances. If he didn't have to concern himself with protecting her, perhaps he'd see her as a desirable woman and ask her out on a real date instead of an outing to please his sister-in-law.

You're becoming a bigger fool every day, Savannah. A man who looks like Chaz can have his pick of women. And you're not going to be one of them.

"What shall I tell her? Are you up to it?"

His question disturbed her taunting thoughts and she shrugged nonchalantly. "Sure. Why not? While I'm here in Austin, I should use the time to get to know some of my Fortune relatives."

He arched a brow at her. "That's something your father is dead set against."

"How would you know such a thing?"

"Miles made his feelings clear when he was interviewing me for this bodyguard job. Then later, when I met your brother Nolan, he mentioned that your father wanted his family to remain separated from the other Fortunes. Although, I have no idea whether he's following Miles's wishes. I only met your brother a few hours before your plane landed in Austin."

She nodded. "I talked to Nolan briefly last night, but we mostly discussed little Stella, and Lizzie, and everyone back home in New Orleans. He didn't bring up Charlotte, or Gerald Robinson, or his giant brood of offspring. And I didn't want to broach the subject. It's too…dismal."

"Well, get prepared. Schuyler will bring up the sub-

ject. She has the grand notion that *all* the Fortunes can
get together and become one big happy conglomeration
of relatives."

Savannah swung her head back and forth. "I doubt
that will ever be possible. Dad and his half brothers—the
ones he learned about a few months ago—all feel very
bitter toward their father, Julius. I can't see that changing. The man hurt a lot of people and, from what I hear,
Gerald has also damaged plenty of lives."

He leaned back in his chair and studied her thoughtfully. "I've tried to imagine what it feels like for you to
be a Fortune, but I can't. No matter where you go, the
Fortune name registers with people. You never have to
worry how you're going to pay the utilities or grocery bill.
Whatever you want, you can go out and buy."

She frowned at the image he was painting. "There are
plenty of things money can't buy or fix, Chaz. And being
a Fortune is not always easy. Like now—with Charlotte
taking aim at us."

"Yeah, I can see where some things about carrying the
Fortune name would be hard to deal with."

She swallowed the last of her spaghetti before she replied, "I think being a Fortune was harder for me and my
siblings when we were children. Classmates teased, and
taunted, and set us apart from them. And even the ones
who were supposed to be good friends stabbed you in the
back. That's why I grew so close to Bethann. She never
treated me any differently. What about you? I'd like to
hear what it's like to be a Mendoza."

A faint smile bent the corners of his lips. "Compared
to yours, the Mendozas are a simple family. We grew up
in Miami and back then, money was mostly tight. We all
worked to get the things we needed."

"Have you always been a close-knit family?"

He inclined his head. "Always. But naturally when you have five young boys together under one roof, there's going to be squabbles and wrestling matches. The Mendoza house had plenty of those."

Smiling, she rested her arms on the table edge and leaned earnestly toward him. "I'm sure your parents were usually around to keep the peace. I can't imagine what it must have been like for your mother. Trying to corral five boys would be crazy."

Like a cloud suddenly covering the sun, his face went dark. "Dad was the one who did all the corralling. See, my parents divorced when we boys were very young. After that, she wasn't ever around. As far as that goes, she still isn't."

"Oh. I'm sorry. I noticed you hadn't spoken of her. I thought she might have died."

He pushed back his chair and carried his plate over to the counter. "No need to be sorry. And no, Mom is still living. Although it's rare that any of us hear from her," he conceded. "My parents had a volatile relationship. Dad liked wine and women. Too many women. Mom took his cheating as long as she could and left. As an adult, I can see it was for the best that they divorced. But as a child, it was hard to understand why our mother wasn't around."

Savannah watched him scrape his leftovers into the garbage disposal while wondering if he'd just revealed a reason why he had no interest in marriage or a long-term relationship.

"Your dad never married again?"

He released a short cynical laugh. "No. Thank goodness. He's still too much of a playboy to settle down with one woman."

Like father, like son? Perhaps Chaz wanted to pursue women without acquiring the baggage of children and a divorce. Or was he simply afraid to take a wife? Afraid she would leave him, like Esteban's had left him?

"Well, it's not like the Fortunes have been blessed with fidelity. Every time I walk by a rack of tabloids, I expect to see another love child of Gerald's plastered on the front page."

He spooned coffee grounds into the coffee machine and added the water before he turned to look at her.

"The Mendozas have had their own scandals," he said flatly. "Not that long ago, my brothers and I learned that Joaquin was actually our half brother. After years of believing he was our cousin, you can imagine how shocked we were. How everyone who knew our family was shocked."

Savannah couldn't believe he was sharing such a private matter with her. Especially after the angry outburst they'd exchanged earlier. She could only think that the argument between them had acted like an icebreaker.

Picking up her plate, she joined him at the counter. "Your cousin actually turned out to be your half brother? How did that happen?"

He rolled his eyes. "How do you think? My father had sex with my uncle's girlfriend."

His blunt explanation put a blush on her face. "I understand that part. You said you learned about Joaquin not long ago. Was it a family secret or something?"

"Or something, I guess you'd call it. Technically, Luz wasn't Orlando's wife at the time she got pregnant. You see, she'd always been in love with my father. But even then, Dad couldn't be a one-woman man. He ran off with another woman before Luz could tell him about the baby. Orlando married her and together they decided to keep secret the fact that Esteban was actually the baby's father."

"Oh, my. What a tangled web. How did the secret finally come out?"

Folding his arms against his chest, he slanted her a rueful glance. "Well, we all knew a deep riff had existed for years between Dad and Uncle Orlando. We just didn't know what had caused it. Until Joaquin wanted to donate blood for his sick mother and discovered his blood type couldn't have been produced by Luz and Orlando. He began putting two and two together and finally confronted Orlando. Once the truth came out, the two men flew to Miami and told Esteban what had happened."

"You mean, after all those years, Esteban still had no idea that Joaquin was actually his son?"

Chaz shook his head. "No. To say it floored him would be putting it mildly. But as it turned out, the two brothers forgave each other and Joaquin is close to both men."

"So now all of you are running Mendoza businesses together," she mused. "Maybe there is hope for the Fortunes to be one big happy family. But that would take a whole lot of forgiving by a whole lot of people."

He slanted her a sly smile and as her gaze met his dreamy brown eyes, the pit of her stomach tumbled end over end.

"Right now, I'm just glad you decided to forgive me."

Because he didn't want to lose his bodyguard job? Or because he wanted to stay here with her?

Like a fool, she wanted to believe the latter.

Chapter Ten

"Savannah, a fairy must have sprinkled pixie dust over you last night," Marva said the next day as the two women made their way to a small break room for coffee. "You've been smiling all morning."

"Why shouldn't I be smiling? It's a lovely spring day outside and these classes are getting easier or I'm getting smarter," she joked.

In truth, Savannah did feel happier than she'd ever felt since arriving in Austin. And she was beginning to wonder if the old adage about making up after an argument was even better than not having an argument in the first place.

Something had happened to Chaz last evening after they'd quarreled. She honestly didn't have a clue as to what or why the change had occurred. She only knew that he'd felt so much closer, so much more willing to share himself with her.

Marva chuckled. "You must be getting smarter, Savannah. I'm still trying to make sense of how one tiny cell of bacteria can turn into an epidemic," she joked.

The two women entered the break room and headed straight to the coffee machine.

"Actually, I'm a bit excited about this evening, Marva. I'm going out to dinner. With Chaz and his brother and sister-in-law."

The older woman cast a doubtful look at Savannah. "You're going out with your bodyguard?"

"Well, it's not like a date. I mean, yes, he'll be guarding me, but it's sort of a family thing, too. You see, Chaz's sister-in-law is my cousin. A few months ago, my family learned about a bunch of relatives we didn't know we had. Many of them live here in Austin."

"Hmm. I've noticed the Fortune name popping up here and there around town. Someone told me that the business magnate that owns Robinson Tech is actually a Fortune."

"That's right. He's my uncle. Or half uncle, I guess you'd say. In any case, I'm not sure I'd ever want to meet him."

Marva frowned. "Why not?"

Savannah waved a dismissive hand through the air. "It's a long story. So long in fact that I only know portions of it. Some day when we're not studying about good and bad bacteria I'll tell you what I do know."

Marva gave her a sly wink. "I'm going to hold you to that promise."

"Hey, ladies. How about some cookies to go with that coffee? Got them fresh from the deli this morning."

Savannah looked around to see Arnold entering the room, waving a white paper bag at them.

"What kind of cookies?" Marva wanted to know.

"I'm not picky," Savannah told him. "I'll take one."

She stirred cream and sugar into her coffee and followed Arnold over to one of the utility tables.

As she started to sit in a chair next to him, the cell phone inside the slash pocket on her skirt began to ring.

Deciding she should check the caller ID to make sure it wasn't any of her family, or Chaz checking on her, she pulled out the phone and glanced at the screen.

Live Oak Lane Apartments. Why would someone with the apartment complex be calling her?

"Excuse me, you two, I need to answer this." Savannah stepped away from the table and pressed the accept button.

"Hello, am I speaking with Savannah Fortune?"

"Yes," she answered cheerfully. "I'm Savannah."

"This is Loretta Baines. I'm the superintendent for Live Oak Lane Apartments. We talked when you took out the lease."

"Yes, Loretta. I've not forgotten how nice and helpful you were. Is there something—"

"You need to come to your apartment now, Miss Fortune," the woman interrupted. "There's been an incident."

The urgency in the superintendent's voice alerted Savannah and sent fingers of fear rippling down her spine.

"Incident?" Savannah repeated, her mind whirling. "I have to be back in class in fifteen minutes. I can't—"

"I'm sorry," she said. "But the police need to speak with you. Your apartment has been vandalized."

Police? Her apartment? What was going on? Where was Chaz?

Something cold and heavy hit the pit of Savannah's stomach as the questions raced through her mind.

"No! That can't be!" She barely managed to mutter the words.

"Please get here as soon as you can, Miss Fortune."

The phone connection went dead in Savannah's ear and the silence broke through the shock that had momentarily frozen her.

"What's wrong, Savannah?" Arnold asked. "You look white."

She looked over to her classmates to see Arnold had risen to his feet while Marva was staring, obviously concerned.

"There's been an emergency at my apartment. I have to go. Now. Will one of you please explain my absence to the professor?"

"Of course," Marva insisted. "We'll take care of it."

Arnold promptly shooed Savannah out the door. "You go, Savannah, and do what you need to do."

Outside the building, Savannah caught a taxi and on the way to the apartment complex, she called Chaz's number several times. Each time the ring sounded odd and his voice mail answered.

Earlier this morning when he dropped her off at the science building, he'd told her he was planning to make a trip to the winery while she was at class. Apparently, there was a problem with his phone, or the signal was spotty in his area. Whatever the reason, she desperately wished she could hear his voice. She needed him now more than ever.

Chaz was working on a security buzzer on the main door leading into the fermenting room when his phone signaled a new text message had arrived.

Figuring one of his brothers was simply saying hello, he finished connecting the electrical wires before he put down his tools and pulled the phone from his pocket.

The number attached to the message didn't register with Chaz. But the content was chillingly clear.

Miss Fortune's apartment has been vandalized.

Oh, God! Savannah! Where was she? Had she gone back to her apartment for something? Had she been harmed? Taken?

Horrible scenarios flashed through his mind as he punched her cell number and waited for the sound of her voice.

No answer!

He trotted down the hallway and was nearly to the main office when Esteban stepped through the door.

"Chaz, I was just coming after you. I've made a fresh pot of coffee and—"

"Later, Dad. Something has happened with Savannah and I have to go. I'll deal with the door alarm later."

Esteban looked horrified. "Savannah? What—"

"I don't know! I'll get in touch with you and Carlo later."

Throughout the drive back to the apartment complex, Chaz continued to ring Savannah's phone, but each time it went to voice mail. He then tried the science building on campus and after a long wait was told she wasn't present in Professor Barcroft's class. The information pushed his fear to outright panic.

Damn it! He should have been on campus or at the apartment. He shouldn't have gone to the winery for any reason.

Chaz realized his thinking was irrational, but he couldn't stop the self-condemning thoughts. Savannah was precious to him. Very precious. If anything had happened to her, he'd never forgive himself. He'd never get over it.

As soon as he turned onto the street running adjacent to Savannah's apartment, he spotted two police cars parked in front of her unit and a small group of onlookers huddled together on a nearby lawn.

Once he found a place to leave his car, he trotted to the

apartment and discovered the door wide open. His heart racing, he stepped inside and was immediately stopped by a police officer.

"Sorry. This is a crime scene," he explained. "Do you have a connection to the victim?"

Victim? Chaz flashed him his identification. "I'm Miss Fortune's bodyguard," he answered. "What's happened here?"

"Sorry," he began again. "You'll have to—"

He didn't wait to hear more. In spite of the bulky frame of the officer, Chaz managed to plow his way forward and into the living room.

Even though part of his gaze registered the upturned furniture, ripped drapes, broken lamps and other damage, Savannah was his main focus. To see her standing in the middle of the shambles, being questioned by two police officers, was like a knife in the chest. Especially when he spotted a track of tears on her cheeks. Yet, the enormity of his relief of finding her here and unharmed was so great his knees went weak.

The police officer who'd been guarding the door suddenly came up behind him. "Sir, you're going to have to leave. This is—"

"My business," Chaz told him bluntly. "I'm her bodyguard."

And I want to be so much more.

The thought was whispering through his head when Savannah suddenly looked up and spotted him.

"Chaz! Oh, Chaz!"

Sobbing openly, she rushed straight to him and flung her arms around his neck.

Chaz gathered her in the tight circle of his arms. "Please don't cry, Savannah. We'll get this mess cleaned up later. You're okay. That's all that matters."

"Oh, Chaz, I don't care about me—or this mess! When you didn't answer the phone, I was terrified. I thought the vandals might've done something to you!"

Tucking her head beneath his chin, he stroked a hand down her silky hair. "I thought the same about you. I thank God you're safe."

She clung to him and Chaz realized her whole body was trembling. He pulled her closer and looked over at the officers, who were regarding the two of them with interest.

"I don't think she can deal with any more of this," Chaz told them. "If you have all the information you need for now, I'd like to take her out of here."

After a quick conference between them, the elder of the two lawmen stepped forward. "Okay, you two can leave. After we finish here, we'll have the superintendent lock up. If you find anything missing, call the police department and let us know. Otherwise, if we get any information on the vandals, we'll contact Miss Fortune."

Chaz seriously doubted they'd hear anything from the police. But he hardly needed them or anyone else to tell him who was behind this malicious act. He had no doubt that this devastation of Savannah's apartment was Charlotte Robinson's work.

He thanked the officer for his consideration and drew Savannah aside and out of the earshot of the three men.

"Savannah, I really don't think it's safe to stay here now. The place is in shambles anyway."

Nodding numbly, she looked at him and Chaz couldn't mistake the fear clouding her eyes.

"I'm not going to argue. I don't feel safe here, Chaz. I'm not sure I'll ever feel safe again," she said, her voice threatening to break from another bout of tears.

Swamped with the need to comfort her, Chaz gently

wrapped his arm around her shoulders. "Come on. Gather up whatever essentials you'll want with you for tonight and we'll get out of here."

A half hour later, they arrived at Chaz's apartment. The living quarters weren't nearly as posh as Savannah's residence at Live Oak Lane, but it was comfortable. And Chaz felt confident that no one had followed them here. Which was somewhat of a relief, but was hardly enough to make him feel completely safe.

If Charlotte had already learned about Savannah's presence in Austin and located her apartment that meant she most likely knew about Chaz, too. The thugs who'd demolished the apartment had obviously known that he, or Savannah, wasn't at home when they'd made their hit.

So how long would it take Charlotte to figure out where Chaz lived? And would she dare to come after them here?

He tried to hide his dire thoughts from Savannah as he helped her to the brown leather couch in the small living room, but she seemed to pick up on them anyway.

"You're worried," she said. "I can see it on your face."

He pressed her hands between the two of his. Her fingers felt cold and her face was as pale as his white shirt.

"I am worried," he said. "About you. You're still shaking. I don't want you going into shock."

She tried to smile, but her lips only managed a wobbly slant.

"Don't be silly, Chaz. I'm just feeling a little cold. I'm okay now. Especially now that we're away from Live Oak Lane. Really."

He wasn't convinced. "Don't move. I'll be right back."

Savannah watched as he picked up the bags they'd brought with them from her apartment and left the room. Once he was out of sight, she leaned her head back against the couch and closed her eyes.

She'd never felt so stupid or shallow in her life. From the moment she'd arrived in Austin and learned that Chaz was her bodyguard, she'd believed the whole issue of her safety had been ridiculous. She'd believed her father had blown everything out of proportion. Now, she had to admit that her father, Chaz, even her brother Nolan had been right. The New Orleans Fortunes were just as much a target for Charlotte as the Austin or Houston branches of the family.

Besides ruining the furnishings in the apartment, many of her personal things had been torn and smashed. The viciousness had appalled her and the invasion of her private space had left her sick to her stomach.

Eventually, her father would have to be told about the break-in and the devastation. But she was going to have to pull herself together before she shared the news with any of her family. For one thing, as soon as her father was told, he'd send Nolan over here and her brother would most likely insist on her moving in with him. And Savannah wasn't about to let that happen. Not only did she want her privacy, but she understood that as newlyweds, Lizzie and Nolan needed theirs also. Savannah would go back to New Orleans before she disrupted their lives.

Footsteps sounded nearby and she opened her eyes to see Chaz returning. A folded patchwork quilt was jammed beneath one arm while he carefully balanced a steaming cup on a saucer.

"Is that for me?"

He placed the drink on a low coffee table, then shook out the quilt and draped it over her legs. "All for you. I want you to get warm and relaxed."

She patted the cushion next to her. "Just sit by me, Chaz. That will be enough to get me warm."

He eased down beside her and handed her the cup. "Drink this. It's hot and sweet."

Since her hands were still trembling, she wrapped them both around the cup and gripped it tightly.

"This doesn't look like coffee," she said, peering curiously at the light brown liquid.

"It's tea. Plain Earl Grey. And before you ask, yes, I do drink hot tea on occasion. It's good for you."

She didn't want anything to drink. All she wanted was to have him close to her. But because he'd gone to the trouble of making it for her, she took a few sips.

"You're good for me, Chaz. After today, I realize that more than ever."

A quizzical look came over his face and then he groaned and shook his head. "Just like I thought. You're in shock. You don't know what you're saying."

She placed the cup back on the coffee table, then reached for his hands. A spurt of joy rushed through her when, instead of pulling away, his fingers curled tightly around hers.

"You're wrong," she told him. "My mind is very lucid."

He was nowhere near convinced. "You've been traumatized."

"Sometimes danger can open a person's eyes. And earlier today, when I couldn't get you on the phone, I was so scared that you were in the apartment when the vandals hit. If you'd been there—if they'd hurt you—I couldn't bear that, Chaz."

His gaze was warm and gentle on her face. "If something had happened to you—" his hands released hers and curled tightly around her shoulders "—it would have been my fault, Savannah. How do you think I could have lived with that kind of guilt?"

"No, Chaz. You can't think that way." Her hands

framed his face, her thumbs reaching out to caress the lean hollows beneath his cheekbones. "And anyway, you're here and I'm here and that's all that matters."

His gaze dropped to her lips and Savannah's heart slowed to an anxious thud. During the drive from her apartment to Chaz's, something had happened to Savannah. Maybe the fear she'd gone through had affected her thinking. Or maybe it was facing the truth about being a target of Charlotte's. Or maybe those things had nothing to do with the way she was feeling. She couldn't put a finger on what had caused the change. She only knew that when she'd looked away from the police officers and saw Chaz standing in the middle of the ransacked apartment, it was like a ray of sunshine had filled her heart.

"You're making things very hard for me, Savannah."

"Not any harder than you've been making them for me."

His face drew closer, until a tiny space was all that remained between their lips.

"I said I wouldn't kiss you again."

"I'm forgetting that you said that," she said boldly. "I'm forgetting everything but the two of us—together— like this."

She closed the gap between their lips and the contact created an instant combustion. Desire shot straight to her brain, wiping away every thought in her mind, except making love to him. And with a tiny moan, she wrapped her arms around his neck and pressed her upper body to his.

Her response was like an accelerant being tossed on a fire that was already raging. The desperate search of his lips rocketed her senses to another dimension, where nothing existed, except for the dark mysterious taste of him, the heat of his body next to hers and his strong arms cradling her close. So close.

Over and over, he kissed her until her swollen lips ached with pleasure and the heat inside her had grown, until it was radiating up and down to every pore, every cell of her body.

The intensity of the embrace was like nothing she'd experienced before and her reactions to him were instinctive, hungry and reckless. She couldn't hide her longing for him. Nor did she want to.

Eventually, his lips parted from hers and he turned his attention to her neck. She closed her eyes and tried to breathe as he pressed tiny kisses against the throbbing pulse at the base of her throat.

Groaning, she let her head fall back to expose the creamy column of her throat. His fingers traced her lips, then marked a downward path over her chin and onto the hollow between her collarbones. All the while, his lips were making tiny circles upon her skin, taunting and teasing her with promises of better things to come. And she wanted every delicious experience he could give her.

At some point, the two of them tilted sideways on the couch, until she found herself lying flat on the cushions with his body partially draped over hers.

As his lips continued on a downward exploration, his hands were everywhere. Stroking her arms and across her rib cage, cupping her breasts, then sliding downward to her hips. When his fingers eventually dipped beneath the hem of her skirt and marched up her bare thigh, she tangled her fingers in his hair and urged his mouth back to hers.

The kiss was hot and all consuming, causing need to stab her from all directions. Her lower body reacted by arching toward his. Somewhere beyond the roaring in her ears, she heard him groan and then the hard bulge of his erection was pressing into the juncture of her thighs, telling her in no uncertain terms how much he wanted to be inside her.

The thought shot her senses to an even higher level of desire and by the time his fingers reached the silky fabric of her panties, she was frantic to have him make love to her. Mindlessly, her hips twisted back and forth against his hand, while the mewing sounds in her throat were like a kitten pleading to be fed.

With one hand, he peeled her panties away, then shoved the folds of her skirt up to her waist. His fingertips gently brushed against the intimate folds between her legs and she waited breathlessly for him to deepen the exploration.

Instead, he tore his mouth from hers and looked down at her. His eyes were glittering with golden flecks of light, turning his gaze molten.

"Chaz—oh, please—make love to me!"

Her choked plea brought his lips back to hers and he whispered against them, "Savannah. My sweet, sweet Savannah."

He kissed her once, twice, and then his head dipped to where his hand was wedging her thighs apart. She was mindless, unaware of his intentions, until his tongue suddenly slipped inside her.

The incredible sensation caused to her cry out and as she felt herself spinning away, her hands latched on to his shoulders and gripped the solid ridges. As though holding on to him would stop her from losing all control. But nothing could stop the wild feelings rushing through her, burning her with exquisite pleasure.

While his mouth tasted her, something deeper inside her began to coil tighter and tighter until she couldn't breathe or think. All she could do was hang on to him and let herself be transported to wonderland.

All too soon, the aching need splintered and wave after wave of pleasure undulated through her body. White-hot stars sprinkled over her, touching every inch of her heated skin. Whimpering and stunned, she shuddered against him.

Just as she floated back to earth, he moved away from her and when she opened her eyes, she realized she was seeing him through a glaze of tears.

The emotional reaction of what had just occurred between them should have embarrassed her. But it didn't. Everything she did with Chaz felt open, and perfect, and right.

Sitting up on the edge of the couch, he thrust his fingers through his hair and stared at the floor. "Savannah. I—I didn't mean for that to happen. I don't know why I let it happen!"

The rapturous glow inside her suddenly turned to icy disbelief and she quickly shoved her skirt back in place. "What are you saying, Chaz? I wanted *that* and more to happen. It still can. I—"

"No! Don't say anymore!" he said gruffly, then rising to his feet, he looked ruefully down at her. "Ever since I met you, I've turned into an idiot."

"Thank you," she said, her voice heavy with sarcasm. "That was my goal from the first moment I laid eyes on you—to turn you into an idiot."

He walked across the room and stood facing a picture window covered with slatted blinds. "Savannah, I understand what's going on, even if you don't."

She shot off the couch and walked up behind him. "Really? What exactly do you understand?"

He turned toward her and the tenderness she saw in his

eyes brought a lump of tears to her throat. Was it crazy to think he might possibly care for her? Or was she the one who'd turned into an idiot?

"You've just gone through a traumatic experience," he said gently. "You're vulnerable and shaken. You think you need me and—"

"I do need you. And not just as a bodyguard. I realize you don't want to hear me say this. But I have to say it. I can't go on without saying it."

His groan was full of frustration as he placed his hands upon her shoulders. "Savannah, you need to think beyond this—well, hot chemistry between us. I'm not a man who could ever fit into your life. I don't have to tell you that your father is expecting great things from you. And that doesn't include hooking yourself up to a man like me."

She frowned. "What do you mean a man like you? As far as I can see, you're a respectable, upright man. And don't you think I should be allowed to choose what sort of man I want in my life?"

"Yes. But you're not thinking clearly right now. Later on, after this ordeal is over and you're back in New Orleans, you'll realize how things between us would've never worked."

He sounded resolute, but Savannah wasn't one to back down or give up. "Because?"

A shuttered look came over his face and he moved a few steps away from her. "I shouldn't have to point out our differences to you, Savannah. Look at you. You're a graduate student studying a subject I can hardly pronounce. Your clothes are designer labels. Mine are off the rack." He used his hand to gesture at the room they were standing in. "This is the type of digs I can afford.

It's respectable and comfortable, but nothing like the luxury of your apartment. Get it?"

"No. As of this moment, your apartment looks a hell of a lot better than mine. And who cares if I have more money than you? Or if my college degree is different than yours? None of that is important."

"Your father cares. And probably the rest of the family. And yes, it is important. I know."

Sensing he was holding something back, she closed the distance between them. "How do you know? You're not telling me something, Chaz. And after what just happened between us, I think I have a right to an honest answer."

Grimacing, he walked over to the couch and sat down. Savannah followed, but was careful to keep a short space between them. The last thing she wanted to do was make him feel as though she were crowding him.

"All right, you asked, so I'll tell you. I was engaged once—a long time ago. We dated all through high school and I thought she was the woman I'd spend the rest of my life with. Even though we still had college ahead of us, we made plans for a future together."

Engaged! Chaz had loved a woman enough to want to marry her? She was jealous and surprised at the same time. "Obviously, something happened between you."

His lips twisted to a bitter slant. "Something *didn't* happen. Like a wedding. Like a future together. I went to college through the ROTC. She went to college in New York."

"You lived in Miami at that time?"

He nodded. "You see, Allison was from a rich family. Not nearly as wealthy as yours, but financially they were far above the Mendozas. Her parents wanted her to have the best of everything and they insisted she attend an elite college where she could study the arts. Now that I look back on it, I figure sending her away had actually been her parents' way of separating us. And they were successful. Trying to keep up a long-distance engagement hadn't worked. But it wouldn't have worked anyway. She eventually confessed that she'd fallen out of love with me."

"But you believe she ended things because she was more in love with her wealthy lifestyle than with you."

"Something like that," he admitted. "Anyway, after the engagement ended I was pretty down about everything. I guess my father could see I'd lost my purpose. He jumped in the middle of me and ordered me to grow up and be a man. He'd advised me that there were plenty of other women in the world to take Allison's place." He let out a cynical snort. "And God knows Dad has made his rounds with most of them."

Savannah desperately wanted to touch him, to hold him tight and assure him that nothing about his past or his family made him any less worthy of the loftiest princess in the world. But she understood it was going to take more than a hug and a few words to make him see this.

"So you grew up by entering the army," she stated the obvious.

"Eight years of growing up. And since then, I've been very careful about the women I've dated. Very cautious not to trust, or care, or give."

But he'd given to her, she mentally argued. Perhaps he wasn't aware that he had, but she was. He'd given her company and conversation. Laughter and tears. Anger and smiles. He'd given her heart something else to dwell on besides the loss of her friend and the years she'd not allowed herself to be a whole woman.

"Surely you don't want to live that way for the rest of your life."

"Why not? It's been working for me."

He wasn't being flippant. He was serious. And that made everything about his words so much worse.

Fighting back a sigh, she glanced over at the couch where only minutes ago, he'd thrilled her with his kisses, his touch.

Was that all he wanted or ever intended to have with a woman? Just physical pleasure with no meaning or emotion attached to it?

She had to think not. Otherwise, her heart was in deep, deep trouble.

Chapter Eleven

For the next three days, Savannah attempted to get her life back on schedule. A difficult thing to do when most of her free time away from the study group was spent trying to convince her family that she was safe and sound. Plus, dealing with getting her things removed from the Live Oak Lane apartment and delivered to Chaz's.

Calling her father and relaying the news about the vandalism hadn't been easy for Savannah. He'd reacted just as she'd expected with an I-told-you-so and a loud demand that she return to New Orleans immediately. To hell with her science studies, he'd shouted, her safety was more important.

In spite of his blustering threats to come after her, Savannah had stuck her feet in the sand. She wasn't about to leave Austin. Not because of her studies, but because of Chaz.

Strange, how she'd come to Texas with nothing more on her mind than furthering her education. Now her studies had turned into a side issue. Chaz had become the most important priority in her life and with each day that passed, she was more and more determined to make him see that the chasm in their lives could be connected. That the two of them were meant to be together.

So far, he'd been keeping a safe distance between them, but she'd been using every subtle trick she could think of to lure him closer. She knew he'd not forgotten the passionate moments they'd shared on his couch. No more than she could forget them. And she was hoping those memories would eat at him, remind him that she was there for him to love, rather than push aside.

A light knock on the open door of the bedroom caused her to turn from the dresser mirror to see Chaz standing just inside the room. He was dressed in black slacks, a crisp white shirt and a red-and-navy-patterned tie. He looked incredibly handsome and she had to fight to keep from walking over and placing her hands on his big broad chest.

"Yes?" she asked. "Are you waiting on me?"

"I'm ready. But there's no need for you to hurry. Carlo and Shuyler will entertain themselves until we get there."

The day of the vandalism, Chaz had called his brother and canceled the planned dinner at La Viña. Schuyler had rescheduled it for tonight and Savannah was looking eagerly forward to the evening. She'd dressed in one of the nicest pieces she'd brought from New Orleans and had taken pains to pin her hair into a sleek French twist.

"I'm nearly finished." She turned back to the dresser and picked up a bottle of her favorite perfume. As she sprayed it lightly on her neck and wrist, she said, "I'm sorry about taking over your bedroom, Chaz. I've been working on finding a new apartment, but I haven't found anything appropriate yet. At least, not a place that has the sort of security you'd like for it to have."

He frowned. "I told you that finding a new apartment is unnecessary. We can use mine until you go home to New Orleans."

And when would that be? The study group was scheduled to last for at least three more weeks. What then? She didn't want to think of leaving Austin and Chaz behind.

She returned the perfume bottle to the dresser top. "I'm not sure how much longer that might be," she hedged. "There might be a chance that I can extend my studies with Professor Barcroft into the summer. If that pans out, it would be a great opportunity for me."

His expression didn't change, making it impossible for her to read his thoughts.

"And what would Miles say to that?" he asked. "He already wants you to pack up and head home. I don't believe he'd be pleased to hear you had plans to remain in Austin a while longer. He might cut off your funds."

Surprised by that remark, she walked over to him. "I hardly need money from Dad to support my studies or living expenses. I have my own."

"Oh. I should've known."

There wasn't exactly sarcasm in his voice, but she could definitely hear a frown. "What does that mean? That I should apologize for being rich?"

"You don't need to apologize for anything," he said bluntly.

She sighed. "Chaz, my mother's parents are wealthy. Not anything like the Fortunes, but they're—let me put it this way—set up very comfortably for the rest of their lives. Anyway, when I was small, my maternal grandfather set up a trust fund for me. I try to use it only when necessary. But if Dad should cut off my funds for some reason, I'm still okay."

"Lucky you."

"No. I'm not lucky, Chaz. I'm blessed," she corrected him. "And I'll tell you something else. I'm not Allison."

His brows shot up. "Who said you were?"

Exasperated, she plucked her designer handbag from the foot of the bed. "You did. In about a thousand ways."

"If this is the kind of night we're going to have," he muttered ruefully, "then I'm really looking forward to it."

She smiled sweetly at him. "Good. Because I happen to think it's going to be a very special night."

He turned to go. "Come on," he said. "Let's get going before Schuyler starts ringing my phone."

La Viña, the family-owned-and-operated restaurant of the Mendozas was located next to the winery. If Savannah hadn't ended up having her little weeping spell in the sculpture garden the day they'd visited the winery, Chaz would've probably shown her through the eating establishment. Instead, they'd gone home and later that night he'd kissed her out on the patio. For as long as Savannah lived, she would remember that exact moment and the thrill that had shot through her when he'd placed his lips on hers.

"The place looks busy," Savannah remarked as Chaz parked the car in a spot reserved for employees. "Is it always like this?"

"Most of the time. Once the public discovered the food was as good as our wine, we've stayed busy. And I think they enjoy getting out of the city proper to dine in a quieter setting."

He helped her out of the car and as they walked to the front entrance, Savannah gazed around at the beautifully landscaped grounds and far-off views of the vineyard. She had no doubt the Mendoza businesses would only continue to grow. From what Chaz had told her, the whole family worked hard to see that everything that needed to be done got done.

Once inside the building, they walked down a short, wide foyer decorated with potted plants, hall trees and two parson benches. Before they reached the end of the foyer they were met by a pretty hostess with bright red hair.

She smiled charmingly at Chaz. "Good evening, Mr. Mendoza. Your family is already here. If you'll follow me, I'll show you where they're seated."

The hostess grabbed two menus and started into the main area of the restaurant. As Savannah and Chaz followed, she wondered if Chaz was noticing the subtle sway of the woman's hips and the way her copper curls brushed against her back.

Had Chaz taken his playboy father's advice and used a long list of women to help him forget his broken engagement? Ever since he'd told her about Allison, she'd been asking herself if she was fighting a losing cause. If Chaz had truly taken after his father, he might be content to remain a bachelor for the rest of his life.

Don't be stupid, Savannah. You've only known the man a short time and you're trying to turn him into husband material. He's already told you he's not the marrying kind. The best you can hope for is a few minutes of passion in his bed. And you might not even get that much.

"Here we are. I'll send the waiter around to see about your drinks."

The hostess interrupted the jeering voice in Savannah's head and she looked up to see Carlo and Schuyler sitting at a rectangular table situated near a pair of French doors that opened to an outside patio paved with flat rock.

"Savannah!" All smiles, Schuyler promptly jumped to her feet and gave Savannah a tight hug. "I'm so happy to see you again!"

"It's nice to see you again, too," Savannah said with genuine affection. Although she'd only met her a few months ago, Savannah could see her Fortune cousin was a truly sincere person. Like Chaz had said, Schuyler wanted everyone to be happy. "I'm glad we could finally meet for dinner tonight."

After Carlo greeted her with a handshake, Chaz helped her into the chair directly across from Schuyler's, while he sat across from his brother.

Once the waiter served them a bottle of Mendoza wine and a tray of hors d'oeuvres, Carlo and Schuyler began to ply them with questions about the apartment break-in.

"This is really so embarrassing," Schuyler said to Savannah. "On the first trip you make to Austin, Charlotte Robinson torches the Robinson estate and nearly kills her own son, who just happens to be your cousin and mine. Now, you come back to Austin and barely have time to get settled when you're personally terrorized by Charlotte. You must be having all kinds of awful thoughts about this branch of Fortunes."

Savannah gave her a wan smile. "Not really. None of Gerald's children can help what their mother does."

Carlo cast his wife an indulgent look. "Schuyler, you're putting the cart before the horse. We're not sure yet if Charlotte was behind the apartment break-in."

"Well, of course she was," Schuyler argued. "A twelve-year-old could figure that out."

Carlo looked at Chaz. "Is that your deduction?"

Chaz shrugged. "There isn't definite proof yet. But there should be soon. Savannah and I got word this afternoon that they caught the two men who vandalized the apartment. Connor Fortunado is busy trying to connect the dots and trace them back to her."

"They're not talking?" Carlo asked, his gaze vacillating between Chaz and Savannah.

"Not yet," Chaz answered. "But if they're squeezed hard enough, they'll spill something. And Connor has other ways of uncovering the information."

Schuyler looked over at Savannah. "I don't know about you, Savannah, but knowing Charlotte is out there plotting and planning against the Fortunes makes me uneasy. Considering the fact that she's already come after you, you must be downright frightened."

The only thing that frightened Savannah now was the reality of Chaz not being in her life. "I'll be honest, the sight of my apartment shook me to the core. But I've gotten over the scare. And I have Chaz to protect me."

Across the table, Carlo and Schuyler exchanged sly glances.

Chaz swigged down a portion of his wine, then cleared his throat. "Savannah has a problem," he said wryly. "She believes I'm some sort of caped crusader who can stop a bullet with his bare hands."

Carlo grinned at Schuyler and from her spot across the table, Savannah could see his eyes twinkling with affection for his lovely wife. If only Chaz could look at her that way.

"Is that how you think of me, honey?"

With a coy laugh, Schuyler placed a hand on her husband's arm. "Always," she said to him, then glanced curiously at Savannah and Chaz. "So how are you two getting along?"

"Schuyler!" Carlo scolded. "You're being way too nosey. I thought you wanted to make a good impression on your cousin."

Before Savannah could say a word, Chaz spoke up in a cool tone. "Savannah and I are getting along just fine. I've drawn a line down the middle of the apartment. She stays on her side and I stay on mine."

His long fingers were casually toying with the stem of his wineglass and to anyone else he might have appeared relaxed, but Savannah was learning there was always something going on behind those dark eyes of his.

"You're really awful, Chaz," Schuyler told him. "I hope you gave Savannah the best part of the bathroom."

"And which part is that?" Chaz asked.

Chuckling, Schuyler glanced knowingly at Savannah. "Forgive my brother-in-law. He's a bachelor. You're going to have to teach him a few things," she said, then leveled a pointed look at Chaz. "The woman has to have the side with the mirror, Chaz!"

Chaz poured more wine into his glass. "Carlo, don't you think it's time you called the waiter over so we can order? I'm starving."

Later that night as Chaz drove the two of them back to his apartment, he noticed that Savannah had gone unusually quiet. Which was puzzling since she'd been very chatty throughout dinner.

"Are you angry with me about something?"

From the corner of his eye, he could see her staring at him.

"No. Why should I be? Dinner was lovely. The food was delicious and the company enjoyable. And the Mendoza wine has me feeling—" she stretched her upper body like a lazy cat and leaned back in the seat "—very warm and relaxed. It's no wonder the winery is running out of merlot."

With a silent groan, Chaz purposely fixed his eyes on

the highway, but the dark asphalt and oncoming head-lights couldn't wipe her beautiful image from his mind. Tonight, she'd somehow managed to look even more gorgeous than usual and all through the evening, he'd found it nigh impossible to keep his eyes off her.

He knew very little about women's clothing, but he'd bet the dress she was wearing cost several months of his salary. The skirt was splashed with pink and yellow roses and made a swishing sound each time she moved. The top part was the same yellow as the roses and it draped over her breasts like a soft cloud. Even in the dim lighting of the car interior, the chunks of diamonds in her ears glittered provocatively with each slight movement of her head. Her hair, which was pinned to the back of her head, was just messy enough to have a man thinking of long hot kisses and sweaty sheets.

"If you found dinner enjoyable, then why aren't you talking about it?"

She sighed. "I suppose because I'm too busy trying to figure what's wrong with me. Or if there's something wrong with you."

His heart jerked, then jumped into overdrive. For the past three days since they'd moved into his apartment, he'd been aware of her subtle taunts. Like wearing shorts that showed more leg than the law should allow and wearing T-shirts without a bra. Oh, yes, he'd noticed. He was surprised he'd not already ground his teeth down to the gums and frozen his skin with all the cold showers he'd taken. But he was determined not to succumb to her seduction. Making love to Savannah would be wrong. It would be inappropriate. But it would also be downright delicious.

"Maybe you should explain."

"As a woman, I'm wondering what I'm lacking. I'm

asking myself just what I need to do to get you to take me to bed."

He sucked in a deep breath and gripped the steering wheel. "You're already sleeping in my bed."

"Because it's the only bed in your apartment, that's why. As far as I'm concerned, we should be sharing it instead of you sleeping on the pullout sofa."

He took his eyes off the road long enough to look at her. Which was a mistake. She was smiling at him, a crooked little smile that melted his bones.

He'd already made love to her hundreds of times in his mind. And on the couch that day of the vandalism... Those reckless moments with her were burned into his brain. The way she'd looked. The way she'd smelled and tasted. She'd turned into a wild, little kitten in his arms. Now the endless thinking, and wanting, and resisting was beginning to exhaust him.

He said, "You think that's what you want."

"It's what you want, too, Chaz," she said, her voice soft and inviting.

He didn't bother to deny it.

By the time they reached Chaz's apartment, the tension between them had grown to the point where one touch would be like lighting a fire beneath an oil derrick. Still, Savannah wasn't sure that one touch would happen. The man had the resistance of a saint. For the past three days, he'd kept his distance in spite of her efforts to entice him. There was no reason she should think tonight would be any different.

Until they stepped inside the apartment.

As soon as he locked the door behind him, his hand reached out and snared her shoulder.

The next thing she knew, his arms were crushing her

to his chest and his lips were fastened over hers in a kiss that ravaged her senses.

The floor beneath her feet began to tilt wildly and, seeking an anchor, she grasped his shoulders. Her fingers clung to the hard warmth while her lips opened wider, inviting him to deepen the kiss even more.

When his tongue slipped inside and tangled with hers, she was certain every bone, every cell in her body was incinerating into ashes. She promptly forgot to breathe and as her knees turned to jelly, she wilted like a flower in the desert sun.

Bending, Chaz swept her up in his arms and carried her through the dark apartment until he reached the bedroom where she'd left a tiny night lamp burning. At the side of the bed, he paused long enough to plant a swift kiss on her lips, before he gently eased her onto the queen-sized mattress.

As soon as he joined her on the bed, Savannah rolled toward him and linked her arm around his rib cage. With her lips against his, she murmured, "This is where you belong, Chaz. Right here with me."

"This is crazy," he argued. "It shouldn't be happening. But I don't want to stop it. I don't want to stop this."

He kissed her lips, his hands delving into her hair, his tongue exploring the sharp edges of her teeth. Savannah instinctively drew herself closer until her body was perfectly aligned with his.

"You have way too many clothes on."

His hoarse voice was enough to cause her toes to curl inside the delicate high heels encasing her feet.

"So do you. Far too many," she whispered. "Don't you think we should do something about it?"

His hands came around to the middle of her back where a zipper fastened her dress. He tugged the zipper pull until the fabric was gaping, allowing him to touch her smooth flesh.

The track of his fingers was like a torch, slowly burning a trail, branding her wherever they went. Savannah endured the sensation for a few seconds before she frantically needed to give him more and take everything he was willing to give her.

Slipping out of his arms, she stood long enough for her dress to slide to the floor. By the time she stepped away from the pool of fabric, Chaz was standing next to her, his hands skimming over the curves and angles of her body.

Before she knew it, her lacy undergarments had joined the dress and she was standing naked before him. In the shadowy light, she could see his eyes devouring her and the hunger in his gaze was as potent as the touch of his hands.

She whispered his name as his head bent and he took one pink nipple into his mouth. Pleasure rippled through her, but it was hardly enough to ease the ache that was building within her.

Awkwardly, she contorted her arms around his head so that her fingers could reach the buttons on his shirt. She'd managed to unfasten two of them when he finally eased back and brushed her hands aside.

"Let me," he said thickly. "It'll be faster."

Once his clothes were out of the way, Savannah was eager to wrap her arms around him and feel his bare skin next to hers. But he detoured the pleasure by easing her onto the bed, then turning his back to her.

"I'm sure you don't have protection with you," he said as he fished through a drawer on the nightstand.

A blush stung her cheeks. "That's not something I normally need."

He glanced over his shoulder at her. "No. I don't expect you do. I'll take care of it."

Only a moment or two passed before he rejoined her on the bed, but to Savannah it felt like forever. She eagerly opened her arms to him and sighed when his bare skin was finally pressed to hers.

When her lips found his, he kissed her tenderly, passionately, drawing emotions from somewhere deep inside her. She recognized that nothing would be right without this man at her side. Loving her like this. Forever.

They were both breathless when he finally eased his lips away from hers. Savannah was still gulping for air, when his head descended to her breasts and his tongue made tantalizing circles around each nipple before drawing one and then the other into his mouth.

She thrust her fingers into his hair and cradled his head with her hands until he got his fill. By then she was on fire for him and the ache between her legs had grown to an unbearable peak.

"I need you now, Chaz! Please—I've waited so long."

His brown eyes glittered down at her. "We've both waited too long," he said, his voice rough with desire.

Bracing his hands near her shoulders, he positioned himself over her. Savannah parted her legs and welcomed him inside.

His entry was swift, and complete, and literally tore the breath from her lungs. A groan lodged in her throat as she gripped his upper arms and waited for the stars inside her head to settle.

"Savannah? Are you okay?"

The whispered question caused her eyelids to flutter open and she looked up at him. The expression in his eyes and on his face was like nothing she'd seen on him before. It was naked, and stark, and so real that tears pooled in her eyes.

He cared. Oh, yes, he truly cared. She couldn't be wrong about that.

"I'm wonderful. I'm incredibly happy."

"That's all I want."

Lowering his head down to hers, he kissed her slowly, tenderly, while at the same time he began to move inside her with the same gentle rhythm.

All at once, a mixture of desire and sweet emotion swirled through her and with a helpless moan, she arched upward, drawing him completely inside of her.

The movement caused his head to snap back and a guttural sound rushed past his lips. Instantly, his strokes quickened and she met each one hungrily, frantically.

On and on they went, locked in a love dance. Until the shadowy room was nothing but a blur, and the only sounds she could hear were the harsh intake of his breaths and the wild drum of blood beating in her ears.

His hands were everywhere, sliding along her sweat-damp skin, driving her desire to the breaking point. And then, just when she thought her whole body was going to burst into tiny pieces, she could feel herself nearing the end of a glittering rainbow. If only she could reach it...

In the back of her mind, she felt her fingers aching and realized she had a death grip on his shoulders. Yet, she couldn't let go. If she did, she would surely float away.

Relief suddenly exploded inside her as wave after wave of incredible sensations washed through her body. At the same time, she felt Chaz's hands gripping her buttocks, lifting her toward his final thrust. And then he was crying her name and burying his face between her breasts.

Several moments passed before he moved his weight off

her and by then Savannah had regained enough strength to roll toward him and snuggle her body next to his.

Beneath her palm, his chest was damp and hot, his heart was thumping madly. As she touched him, she realized she loved the sensation of his skin against her fingertips, the scent of him filling her head. He made her drunk with desire. He made her feel as though she could conquer the world. That with him at her side, her life would be complete.

And that was because she loved him. Loved him with every fiber of her heart. Nothing had ever been as clear in her mind as her feelings were at that moment.

"It's my turn to ask if you're okay," she asked huskily.

His head turned slightly toward her and though one corner of his mouth lifted with amusement, she could see the expression in his eyes was serious.

"I've never been *this* okay, Savannah." He turned onto his side and pushed a hand into her tangled hair. As he swept the strands away from her face, he swallowed and closed his eyes. "I'm not sure what it means. Except that we have something special together. Very special. And I don't want to give it up."

Tears of joy spilled onto her cheeks. "We are meant to be together, Chaz. Now and always."

He opened his eyes and looked into hers. "If your father finds out about this, it could be very bad. For both of us."

"He's not going to find out. How could he? We're not going to tell him, or anyone else. Not until we're ready." She reached over and traced a fingertip down one side of his mustache and on to the corner of his lips. "We're grown adults, Chaz. This is nobody's business but ours."

Groaning, he rested his cheek against hers. "And that's the way we're going to keep this relationship. Just between you and your bodyguard."

Chapter Twelve

By the middle of the next week, Savannah felt like she was waltzing on the top of the world and her happiness must have shown. Marva was eyeing her with a speculative grin, while Arnold wanted to know what she'd been eating to put such a glow on her face.

As Savannah and her two college friends sat eating their lunch in an atrium connected to the science building, Marva said, "For a woman who had her apartment vandalized and half her things destroyed, you sure have bounced back quickly."

With a good-natured smile, Savannah shrugged. "I'm not one to let troubles get me down. My parents always taught us kids that adversity makes a person stronger."

And it helped to have the man you love with you through every step, good or bad, Savannah thought. But her feelings about Chaz were something she couldn't reveal to anyone. These past few days, he'd continually warned her that Charlotte's spies could be anywhere among them and for her not to speak to anyone about their relationship. Not because he was ashamed of the fact that they were lovers, but because he feared the information might be picked up and passed on to the wrong person. Particularly, her father.

If Miles did discover Savannah had been sleeping with her bodyguard, he'd blow a gasket, especially with her. As for Chaz, she wasn't sure how her father would deal with him. And she didn't want to know.

She and Chaz needed time, Savannah thought. More time to develop the bond that was growing deeper between them with each passing day. So far, she'd not yet mentioned the *love* word to Chaz. Not because she had doubts or questions about her feelings for him. She knew, with everything in her heart, that she loved him and would love him for the rest of her life. But she'd held the word back from him, mostly because she wasn't convinced he was ready to hear such a vow from her. And the last thing she wanted to do was make him feel pressured or boxed into something he wasn't ready for.

"Well, I can tell you one thing," Arnold said, as he dug into a bag of cheese puffs. "If someone broke into my apartment and destroyed it just to give me a warning, I'd be getting the heck out of Dodge. You have to be one brave woman, Savannah."

Chuckling, Savannah shook her head. "Not really, Arnold. I'm just stubborn. Why would I want to leave now when I'm just beginning to like Professor Barcroft?"

Marva shot her an incredulous look. "Are you kidding? I'd like to tell him just how much of a weirdo he is!"

"Well, from what everyone tells me, you have to be a bit of a weirdo to live in Austin," Arnold said. "Do you think I fit in?"

Marva rolled her eyes toward the gold satin blazer covering his striped shirt. "Perfectly."

Chuckling, Savannah began to gather the leftovers of her lunch and tossed them into a trash basket. "If you two will excuse me, I need to check in with my bodyguard. Since the break-in, he wants to make sure all is safe. If I don't call, he'll start worrying."

"Better hurry," Arnold said. "We only have fifteen minutes before we have to be back to the lab."

Savannah gave him a thumbs-up sign. "I won't be late."

Pulling the strap of her handbag onto her shoulder, she walked to the far end of the atrium where she was out of earshot of her friends and the few other students who were relaxing in the sunny plant-filled room.

Chaz's number was at the top of the contact list on her phone and her heart picked up its pace at the thought of hearing his voice. Calling him at lunchtime each day had started because of the break-in, but since their relationship had turned physical, the calls had evolved into a romantic connection that she looked forward to.

With the phone to her ear, she eased onto a cushioned chair and waited for Chaz to answer.

When he didn't pick up, she waited and tried again. There was no answer the second time, or the third, or fourth.

The common-sense part of her brain reasoned that Chaz's phone wasn't working, or the signal tower had lost power. Or he could have his hands too busy to answer. Any number of things could prevent him from answering. But the intuitive part of her brain had the sickening feeling that something was wrong. But what? Had Charlotte's thugs been trailing him? Had they caught up to him and harmed him in some way?

Uneasy, she slipped the phone back into her purse and glanced up to see Marva waving at her.

"Is something wrong, Savannah?"

She bounced up from the chair and hurried to catch up with the woman. "I'm not really sure, Marva. Chaz isn't answering."

"Well, I wouldn't get all panicky about that. He's probably busy or away from his phone."

His phone was a connection to his security responsibilities with the winery and the restaurant. Not to mention the fact that it was a safety link between her and Chaz throughout the day. No. He wouldn't be without his phone. But she didn't bother to explain all of this to Marva.

"I hope you're right. Since the ordeal with my apartment, I see how things can change in an instant. And the person who we think is responsible for the break-in hasn't been caught. I worry about Chaz's safety."

Marva gave Savannah's arm a reassuring pat. "You need to remember he's a bodyguard. He knows how to keep himself out of trouble. Besides, it's his job to worry about you. Not the other way around."

That was true, but Marva didn't have the whole picture. Chaz was the man she loved. The man she intended to spend the rest of her life with. How could she not worry about him?

"I've already missed a few hours of lab because of the apartment break-in. It wouldn't be good to miss more," she mumbled worriedly, "And I'm probably being silly to worry. Still, I wish I could go check on him."

"Then go," Marva told her. "I'll email all my notes to you later and you can go over them before tomorrow's lab."

She gave the older woman a tight hug. "Oh, Marva, you're wonderful. I love you."

Marva chuckled. "I'm not wonderful. Arnold calls me Austin-weird."

Doing her best to push aside her unease, Savannah linked her arm through Marva's. "Come on, we'd better get back to the lab. Chaz will be here to pick me up this evening. I'll find out then why he isn't answering the phone."

However, that evening Chaz wasn't there to pick up Savannah at their usual meeting spot behind the science building. The park bench was empty and there was no sign of his car anywhere.

A sick feeling washed over her as she stood looking helplessly around the parking lot. Oh, God, her instinct earlier in the day had been right. Something was wrong. Awfully wrong! But what? If he'd been hurt, someone would've surely contacted her by now.

She continued to ring his phone, but the only answer she got was a recorded voice informing her that the party she was calling was not available. Which could only mean his phone was turned off. But why? Chaz would never do that intentionally.

"Miss Fortune?"

The male voice calling her name caused Savannah to whirl around to see a huskily built, middle-aged man with burred brown hair striding toward her.

She froze in her tracks. Could he be one of Charlotte's muscle men? Her gaze darted to either side of the walkway. There was no place for her to run. And Chaz wasn't here to protect her!

The man must have recognized the terror on her face because he suddenly called out to her again. "Don't be frightened. I was sent here by your father, Miles."

The use of her father's name was hardly enough to convince her not to bolt. But she stood her ground and waited until he halted a few steps away from her.

"Who are you? Where is Chaz?" she demanded.

"My name is Greg Anderson. Mr. Fortune just hired me as your new bodyguard," he said bluntly. "And instructed me to pick you up here."

New bodyguard? That couldn't be possible! Or…could it?

She raked a skeptical glance over the man. "I don't believe you!"

His expression turned exasperated and sheepish at the same time, which made Savannah doubt his credibility even more. But at least he wasn't attempting to grab her and hustle her away to a waiting vehicle, she thought.

He said, "Then I suggest you call your father and confirm my identity."

"You haven't answered my question about Chaz," she stated sharply.

He shook his head. "If you're talking about your prior bodyguard, I don't know anything about him. But I'm sure your father will explain everything."

She hardly wanted to get into a heated conversation with her father now. Not here on the sidewalk with this strange man listening to every word. But she didn't have much choice. It would be irresponsible of her to simply trust Greg Anderson without checking with her father first.

With one eye warily on him, she pulled her cell phone from her purse. But before she could punch the call button beneath her father's name, she noticed a new text message from him had just arrived. She quickly scanned the brief message informing her that he'd hired a new bodyguard, Greg Anderson. An accurate description of the man followed, along with the name of the reputable security company that Mr. Anderson worked for.

Slipping the phone back into her purse, she said, "My father has just informed me about hiring you. But I still want to see your identification before I go anywhere with you," she told him.

He promptly obliged by handing her several pieces of ID. Once Savannah was satisfied that everything matched the information her father had messaged her, she reluctantly agreed to leave the campus with him. But all the while, her mind was whirling with questions about Chaz.

When they arrived at Chaz's apartment, she could see his vehicle wasn't parked behind her rental car. The fact only added to her anxious state of mind.

"Is this where you live?"

"Yes," she answered. "The apartment belongs to Chaz Mendoza—the man who's *supposed* to be my bodyguard."

Not waiting around to hear his reply, she hurriedly climbed out of the SUV and let herself into the apartment. As she walked through the small living room, she was relieved to see that no other act of vandalism had occurred. Everything was neat and in its place. But there was no sign of Chaz.

The kitchen held no sign of him and she moved on to the bedroom. Inside the room, her gaze automatically landed on the bed, where early this morning, they'd made slow, sweet love. Everything had been perfect. Chaz had been perfect.

Sighing, she glanced away from the bed and on to the chest of drawers. The grooming items he normally kept there were missing, along with an army duffle bag that hung from a hook on the back of the door.

Had he left? Without a word? The possibility scram-

bled her brain. When he'd dropped her off at the science
building this morning, he'd kissed her goodbye and suggested they go out for dinner this evening. Nothing about
this made sense.

Dazed, her heart pounding, she walked around the
bedroom and tried to calm herself enough to think.
Where could he be? What could have happened?

Questions were shooting through her brain, when she
spotted a small piece of paper lying among her personal
items on the dresser. He must have propped the note
against a perfume bottle, but it had slipped, causing her
to nearly miss seeing it.

Grabbing it up, she began to read:

Savannah,

*I'm not sure how, but your father has found out
about the two of us. He's terminated my services
and hired a new bodyguard to take my place. He's
also threatening a lawsuit against me for breaching
my responsibilities. Whether he goes through with
his threat means little to me. I only want what's best
for you. And I can see that getting out of your way
and out of your life is the only way to achieve that.*

*I'll be gone for the next few days to give you
plenty of time to find another apartment and move
your things.*

Chaz

Her father knew about her and Chaz? And Chaz had
just left without even challenging her father? He wasn't
going to fight for her and everything they had together?

She didn't want to believe either of the two men had
behaved so irrationally and as she began to pace around
the room, anger at both of them overwhelmed her. She

wanted to call her father and scream at him. She wanted to ask him why he thought he had the right to ruin her life. But flinging angry words at him wasn't going to fix things. It wasn't going to tell her where to find Chaz. And right now, that was her first priority.

"I don't know what the situation was with you and Mr. Mendoza, but obviously we can't stay here. We'll have to find another place."

She looked around to see Chaz's replacement standing in the open doorway, watching her. The sight of him made her want to scream. But she tamped down the impulse and said in a clipped voice, "I won't be staying with you any place, Mr. Anderson."

Brushing past him, she hurried to the living room and dug her cell phone from her purse. Someone had to know where Chaz had gone.

Nearly fifteen minutes later, she finally managed to speak to his father, Esteban. She could tell from the man's evasive answers that Chaz had instructed him to keep his whereabouts quiet, a fact which frustrated Savannah even more.

Fighting back tears, she said, "Mr. Mendoza, I admit that I've caused this trouble for Chaz. Or at least, part of it. But he shouldn't have left like this. We can fix this together."

"I think it's time you started calling me Esteban, don't you? Seeing that you're going to be a part of the family."

Where had Esteban gotten that idea? She couldn't imagine Chaz saying any such thing to him. He'd not even come close to telling Savannah that he loved her. And he'd certainly not talked about spending the rest of his life with her.

Had Esteban just cleverly put two and two together and come to his own conclusion that Chaz and Savannah had become lovers? Had he said as much to some of the family or a friend? Was that how word had gotten to her father?

She bit down on her lip as tears gathered in her eyes. "Esteban, I think you're too much of a romantic to see the situation clearly."

His chuckle was full of affection. "I know my son well. The only reason he left town is because he cares for you. And now that I see you feel the same way about him I'll tell you that he's gone to Red Rock to visit our relatives there."

Red Rock. She'd never heard of the place. "Thank you, Esteban. Tell me how to get there."

Maria and Jose Mendoza were distant cousins of Esteban and Orlando, but to Chaz they were more like grandparents. For many years, the older couple had lived in Red Rock, where they owned the famed restaurant, Red. The town was an hour away from San Antonio and far enough away from Austin for Chaz to consider the place a refuge. However, he didn't expect to stay here any longer than it took for Savannah to vacate his apartment.

It wasn't until late last night, after Chaz had arrived in Red Rock, that he'd learned exactly how Miles had discovered Savannah was cavorting with her bodyguard. Exhausted, Chaz had been getting ready to climb into bed when Connor Fortunado had called. Not necessarily to discuss Charlotte Robinson with him, but rather to apologize. Shockingly, the crafty private investigator had been the one who'd given Miles the information.

Why had Connor done such a thing? The Fortunes and Mendozas were so closely intertwined. Why cause trouble between them?

Their conversation had been lengthy, but eventually

Connor had managed to explain how he'd been caught between a rock and a hard place. Only two days ago, he'd discovered Charlotte had planted a spy among the La Viña employees. Apparently, a young woman, whose name Chaz hadn't recognized, had overheard Esteban talking with Carlo about Chaz and Savannah and how he was certain the two were already lovers. Upon learning this tidbit, Charlotte had ordered her snoop to spread the word to the people it would hurt the most. Through a mole of his own, Connor had managed to foil the plot. But he'd felt honor bound to relay the information to Miles.

Chaz should have been furious with both men. His father for talking out of turn and Connor for not burying the information. But hell, how could he get angry over the truth? He had been sleeping with Savannah and the fact would've come out sooner or later anyway.

Now, Miles would most likely throw a lawsuit at him, but what the legal ramifications of that might mean for Chaz's financial future, or his reputation as a bodyguard, he could only speculate. Besides, Chaz didn't give a damn about the misery Miles might inflict on him. It was Savannah, and only Savannah, that concerned Chaz now.

Since his abrupt departure from Austin yesterday, his feelings had alternated between guilt and emptiness. He'd tried not to imagine how she must have felt when she'd discovered his note. Hurt, betrayed, angry? As lost as he was feeling this very moment? Or had she sat down and recognized the reality of the situation? She was a Fortune. She deserved a man far better than him. She needed a man in her life that her father would be proud to introduce as his son-in-law.

Oh, God, the pain of giving her up was tearing at his insides, making it nearly impossible to down a bite of food. But Maria was determined to take care of that problem by preparing him one of his favorite meals for lunch.

Now, as she placed a steaming plate in front of him, he tried to give her a grateful smile. "Thanks, Maria. You shouldn't have gone to the trouble."

"It's never trouble preparing a meal for the people I love. So eat. And I mean every bite," she ordered, while pointing to the pile of refried beans, rice and tamales smothered with longhorn cheese.

"I'll try," he promised.

"Don't try. Do it. Good food always makes a person feel better."

She filled herself a plate and eased into the chair next to his. Chaz glanced down the table to the spot where her husband usually sat.

"Where's Jose? Isn't he going to eat?"

"He went down to Red to see if the waitresses had noticed any strangers coming in today. He doesn't want anyone coming into town and ambushing you."

In spite of his misery, Chaz tried to smile. "That's thoughtful of him to be so concerned, but it isn't necessary, Maria. I'm going to have to face up to Miles Fortune sooner or later. I came down here to see you because— well, I need to separate myself from Savannah until she can move out of my apartment."

Maria slanted a wise glance in his direction. "And what if she doesn't move out? You might just have a woman on your hands."

He'd fought his attraction for Savannah long and hard. And even after he'd succumbed to her charms, he'd done so, knowing that making love to her was akin to playing with a tiger. Sooner or later, he was bound to get mauled.

But now, it was more than sex, more than the carnal

needs of his body filling him with torment. Like a blind fool, he'd fallen in love with Savannah.

"That's not going to happen, Maria. I expect Savannah has already packed up. She's probably spent most of the morning calling around the city, searching for a suitable apartment."

"And what about her father? Do you think he'll go to Austin and take her home?"

"No. Miles has already hired a bodyguard to replace me. Apparently, he understands how important Savannah's studies are to her and won't interrupt her time with the study group—unless he believes I'm trying to come back into her life. And that's not going to happen."

Maria gave him a calculated glance as she reached for her tea glass. "I'm sorry to hear that, Chaz."

His fork paused halfway to his mouth. "Sorry? Why? Surely you can see what a mismatch we are."

"I can't see anything—except for the pain on your face. How do you expect to fix that?"

His gaze dropped to his plate. "Time will take care of it."

Maria frowned. "If I lost Jose, no amount of time would fix things."

"That's because you and Jose have been together for many years. The two of you are connected at the hip."

"I have a feeling you're connected to Savannah, too. Much more than you know."

His face stoic, he used his fork to cut a piece of tamale. He shouldn't have come here to spend time with the Red Rock Mendozas, he decided. Everyone in the family was aware that Maria was a hopeless romantic and a matchmaker to boot. Rather than helping him get past this painful ordeal with Savannah, she wanted him to patch things up and fight Miles for his daughter's hand.

The woman just didn't have a clue what a mountainous task that would be. Not just because of Miles. Hell, he wasn't even sure Savannah loved him.

The sound of the doorbell broke into his troubled thoughts and he looked up to see Maria rising from the chair.

"You stay put and eat," she ordered. "I'll go see who could be calling right at lunchtime."

Chaz was forcing himself to swallow down the food when he picked up the sound of voices coming from the front part of the house. Apparently, Maria had company. Which wasn't at all surprising, since both she and Jose had made many friends through their restaurant and years of being Red Rock residents.

A few minutes passed and, deciding it might be a while before Maria returned to the kitchen, Chaz finished the last of the tamales. He was standing at the sink, about to scrape his plate into the garbage disposal, when the sound of footsteps approached the arched doorway leading into the kitchen.

He glanced over his shoulder and very nearly dropped the plate. Maria's unexpected guest was the woman who'd taken up residence in his heart!

"You have a visitor, Chaz," Maria said with a beaming smile. "She's come all the way from Austin to see you."

His gaze gobbled up Savannah's image, while shards of pain sliced through his heart. What was she doing here? To tell him what a coward he was, or that she was going home to New Orleans where she'd never have to see his face again?

Feeling as though he were in a dream, he watched her walk toward him. She was wearing the same pink sundress she'd worn the day he'd taken her to the winery. He'd given her the rose that day and when he'd found her in the sculpture garden with tears in her eyes, it had been impossible not to pull her into his arms.

He'd fallen in love with her that day. And just like that moment, he was finding it a hell of a battle not to go to her and drag her into his arms.

"Hello, Chaz," she said. "You look surprised to see me."

"I am. Did you come here alone?"

She shook her head. "No. My *other* bodyguard insisted on accompanying me. He's waiting out in the living room."

"I see. Well, at least you've been protected since I left Austin." He lowered the plate to the sink, then stepped slightly toward her. "I told my father not to tell anyone where I was. He talks far too much."

"Don't be angry with Esteban. I forced him to tell me."

"Yeah, I'm pretty sure you twisted his arm against his back," he said, then muttered under his breath, "He never could resist a beautiful woman."

Maria's dark eyes were full of approval as her gaze went from Chaz to Savannah and back to Chaz.

She said, "I've been telling Savannah how back in 2005, my daughter Gloria married Jack Fortune and in 2009, my son Roberto married Frannie Fortune."

Chaz didn't want to be reminded. "Savannah already knows about the Fortune/Mendoza weddings."

"Does she know that each year, for the past few years, a Fortune and a Mendoza have gotten married?" Grinning, the older woman sighed as though she were a newlywed herself. "Something magical happens when the two families meet."

"Magic," he repeated dazedly. "Is that what you call it, Maria?"

"Magic. Love. Fate. I think all of those things have touched you, Chaz." She gestured toward Savannah.

"Don't you think you should give your lady a proper hello, Chaz?"

Unable to tear his gaze away from her lovely face, he said, "Hello, Savannah."

She stepped toward him and the tenuous thread holding Chaz's emotions in check suddenly snapped. He reached for her and she fell sobbing into his arms.

"Well now, that's more like it," Maria said happily. "The magic of love has touched both of you two. I can see I need to have a talk with Savannah's father just so he understands that it will do him no good to mess with fate."

Swiping at the tears on her face, Savannah looked at Maria and smiled. "What my father thinks doesn't matter. It's what I know that counts." She looked up at Chaz, her eyes soft and tender. "I love you, Chaz. And all I want is for us to be together."

As Maria discreetly slipped from the room, Chaz attempted to reason with Savannah. "I left Austin because I don't want to ruin your life. Or ruin your relationship with your father."

Shaking her head, she argued, "The only way you could ever ruin my life is for you not to share yours with me. As for my father, he can be unbending at times, but in the end he's a reasonable man. We'll change his mind about us, Chaz. Once he gets to know you, like I know you, he'll be proud we're together."

Chaz needed to believe her. He wanted to tell her how much he adored her and wished to spend the rest of his life with her. But he couldn't. Not until he faced Miles Fortune.

"He might still slap me with a lawsuit," he said.

"If he fights you, he'll be fighting me, too. He'd never hurt me that way."

Chaz wasn't so sure. But he was sure of one thing: he didn't want to live without this woman in his arms.

"All right, Savannah, I'll show you I'm not a coward. How soon can we get to New Orleans?"

With a happy little cry, she rose on her tiptoes and kissed his lips. "We'll drive to Austin, catch a plane and be in New Orleans by dinner tonight."

When Chaz and Savannah finally arrived at the Fortune mansion in New Orleans, the family was in the midst of dinner. Rather than disrupt the meal, they chose to go to the study and wait for Miles to join them.

Even though Chaz had insisted he wanted to meet with the man alone, Savannah firmly refused to leave his side. As the two of them sat close together on a leather couch, their hands tightly entwined, Savannah said, "Dad needs to see us together and get used to the idea that we're a couple. And that we're going to remain a couple."

Skeptical, he looked at her. "You might hear things you don't want to hear."

"Chaz, I'm not a child. I understand that dealing with family matters can be tough. Besides, Dad might hear his daughter say things he doesn't want to hear. But it's high time he heard them."

The remark had barely gotten out of Savannah's mouth when, without a knock, or any warning signal, the door of the study flew open. Miles stalked into the room and, without giving them so much as a cursory glance, headed straight toward the executive chair behind his desk.

Savannah said, "Hello, Dad. I want to introduce you to Chaz."

Polite manners were forgotten as Miles merely took a seat and stared at the two of them. His jaw was clenched, his lips pressed into a straight, angry line. If he'd been any man other than Savannah's father, Chaz would've already pointed out to him that rudeness held no part in being a gentleman.

"That's hardly necessary, Savannah. Mr. Mendoza and I have talked on several occasions." His eyes narrowed to slits as he turned his attention on Chaz. "I had hoped that yesterday would be the last time I'd have to deal with you. For your own sake, you need to leave my house. Now!"

Unflinching, he said, "I'm sorry you feel that way, Mr. Fortune. I was hoping you might be able to meet me with some civility."

Glaring at him, Miles snorted. "You expect civility? After your betrayal? I'll say one thing for you, you're not lacking nerve."

Incredulous, Savannah stared at her father. "Did you honestly think I'd fall in love with a man who wouldn't have the courage to face you? It takes more than having millions of dollars to be a man, Dad."

Miles's face turned a bright red. "Savannah, you've always been one of my smartest children. I thought you'd have the sense to fall in love with a man of your own standing. Instead, you've behaved like a rebellious teenager, sneaking around with a punk from the wrong side of the tracks."

Savannah's jaws snapped shut and when Chaz recognized she was about to jump to her feet, he laid a hand on her arm to hold her back.

"Let me handle this, Savannah." He left her side and walked over to stand in front of Miles's desk. "Sir, I'm going to ignore the name calling because if you honestly considered me a punk, you would've never hired me to protect your daughter."

Miles spoke through clenched teeth, "I obviously made a mistake in judgment."

"I don't think so. I don't believe you ever misjudge anyone. That's why you're so successful at what you do."

Chaz's remark appeared to catch Miles off guard for a moment, but the man was hardly ready to relent.

"Soft-soaping me will get you nowhere. You're not good enough to even look at my daughter—much less—"

When Miles words sputtered, Chaz broke in. "I'm well aware of the stark differences between Savannah and myself. She isn't blind to them, either. But, in spite of our differences, we care about each other."

"I don't give a damn about how either of you feel! In a few weeks, all of that will be dead ashes. Probably sooner. As I've not yet ruled out suing your ass!"

Determined to show Miles he could be cool under fire, Chaz called on every ounce of his military discipline to keep his temper at bay. "If you feel that suing me would fix things as you seem to want them, then go ahead and sue me. But I doubt you'll get anywhere with that threat. Savannah is a grown woman, a consenting adult. In spite of what you might think, you don't control her anymore."

Miles practically shouted, "I'm her father! She lives in my house. Spends my money! If—"

Savannah instantly appeared at Chaz's side and interrupted her father with a scathing retort. "If that's how you think of your children, as puppets you can maneuver with your money, then you're not the father I always believed you to be."

"Savannah, you need to stay out of this!" he warned.

Chaz curled his arm around the back of Savannah's waist and the connection was like a soothing balm to the turmoil inside him. Touching her calmed every doubt he'd ever had about himself. She wasn't like Allison. She wasn't like any of the superficial women he'd dated over the years. She would always stand up for him. Moreover, she would never desert him.

"Mr. Fortune, if you'll take a moment to really consider what taking me to court would accomplish, I believe you'll understand that if you do go through with your threat, you'll also be dragging your daughter right along with me. I can't imagine you wanting to muddy her name and reputation in such a way."

The livid anger on Miles's face slowly began to recede and then his shoulders slumped back against the chair. "No," he admitted gruffly. "I don't want to hurt my daughter."

"Dad, you are hurting me by not seeing Chaz as the wonderful man that he is."

Miles's doubtful glance darted from Savannah to Chaz, then back to her.

"What has Chaz Mendoza done with his life that makes you think he's so wonderful? Damn it all, he's a bodyguard! He makes a living with his muscles."

"You're wrong about that, Dad. In so many ways," she said, her voice soft but resolute. "In the first place, there's nothing wrong with a man using his muscles to make a living. Millions of them do it every day. Secondly, he and his family run very profitable businesses in Austin, with plans to expand. But more importantly, when Chaz looks at me, he doesn't see dollar signs. He sees me for me. He sees a woman who wants to make a positive difference in people's lives. A woman who wants to love and be loved. And have a family of her own with the man of her own choosing."

Miles folded his arms across his chest as his doubtful gaze encompassed the both of them. "I'm not convinced."

Chaz said to him, "Sir, I spent eight years in the army

convincing my superiors that I had what it takes to stand up and fight, to face the enemy, no matter who or what that enemy might be. I don't expect a few words to convince you. Give me a chance and over time I can prove to you that I'm worthy of your daughter."

Miles rose to his feet. "I suppose every person deserves one chance. I'm willing to give you that much. But don't go getting the idea that winning my blessings will be easy. I'm not easy. And I figure you'll throw in the towel long before I am convinced. But we'll see."

With that, he walked past them and out of the study.

Once the door shut behind him, Chaz looked over to see Savannah's eyes were misty, but she was smiling and that was enough to lift the sober weight in Chaz's heart.

"See. I told you we could deal with Dad." She stepped closer and wrapped her arms around his waist. "Let's head back to Austin. Ready?"

He lowered his head and kissed her. "I'm ready to go anywhere with you."

The next night as the two of them lay cuddled together on Chaz's bed, he pillowed Savannah's head and stroked his fingers through her damp hair.

The thrill of making love to her would never dim, he realized. Nor would his love ever fade. With each day, each hour he spent with her, the feelings in his heart grew deeper and stronger.

Today, while she'd been at work with the study group, something she fully intended to finish, he'd made a trip downtown to a jewelry store. After some long thought, he'd decided that a woman who loved camellias would like an engagement ring with an antique flavor. For now, the large square diamond and open scroll setting of yellow gold was hidden away in a velvet box in the nightstand.

When the situation with her father was settled and the ongoing threat with Charlotte was over, Chaz would surprise her with the ring and a marriage proposal. In the meantime, it was enough that the two of them were together and their love for each other had proven too strong for Miles Fortune to break.

"Do you know what I'm thinking?" he murmured against the top of her fragrant hair.

"Mmm. Probably that you're hungry and that we need to go to the kitchen and see what we can find in the fridge."

Chuckling, he pulled her tighter against his side. "No, my sweet, the only thing I'm hungry for is you. I'm thinking how very much I love you."

Her head tilted back to look at him and her eyes filled with wonder. "That's the first time you've ever said that to me."

"I waited so that it would mean something. So that you wouldn't think I was mouthing the words just to please you."

"I did want to hear them," she admitted. "But I want to know that they're real and coming from your heart."

He picked up her hand and brought her fingers to his lips. "They're real, all right. My heart is yours and only yours. For always, Savannah. So you might as well get ready to have a bodyguard for the rest of your life."

With each word he spoke, the smile on her lips grew wider. "And a bunch of little Mendozas to make our family complete?"

He kissed her forehead, her cheeks and finally her lips. "Mmm. At least two or three babies. Maybe even four. What do you think your father will say about that?"

She chuckled. "What can he say? He can't argue with fate. Like Maria prophesied, when a Mendoza and a Fortune get together, something magical happens."

* * * * *

Look for A Fortunate Arrangement
by Nancy Robards Thompson
the next book in The Fortunes of Texas:
The Lost Fortunes
On sale May 2019,
wherever Harlequin books
and ebooks are sold.

And catch up with the previous books
in The Fortunes of Texas:
The Lost Fortunes

A Deal Made in Texas
by Michelle Major

Her Secret Texas Valentine
by Helen Lacey

Texan Seeks Fortune
by USA TODAY *Bestselling Author*
Marie Ferrarella

Available now!

After the walk on the beach, she'd become overly polite and distant. Knowing he wasn't going to sleep, Noah sat up and tossed back the sheets. He found a pair of shorts and slipped them on. Barefoot, he unlocked the screen door and walked out into the night. He saw something out of the corner of his eye and spied someone sitting on the beach. A full moon lit up the night, and as he made his way down to the water, he couldn't stop smiling.

She glanced up at him and smiled. "It looks as if I'm not the only one who couldn't sleep."

Noah sank down next to her on the damp sand. Even in the eerie light, he could discern that the sun had darkened her skin to a deep mahogany. "I was never much of an insomniac before meeting you."

Viviana pulled her legs up to her chest and wrapped her arms around her knees. "I'm not going to accept blame for that."

"Can you accept that I'm falling in love with you?"

Her head turned toward him slowly, and she looked as if she was going to jump up and run away. "Please don't say that, Noah."

"And why shouldn't I say it, Viviana?"

"Because you don't know what you're saying. You don't know me, and I certainly don't know you."

Don't miss
Dealmaker, Heartbreaker *by Rochelle Alers,*
available May 2019 wherever
Harlequin® Special Edition books and ebooks are sold.

www.Harlequin.com

HSEEXP0419R

Looking for more satisfying love stories with community and family at their core?

Check out **Harlequin® Special Edition** and **Love Inspired®** books!

New books available every month!

CONNECT WITH US AT:

Facebook.com/groups/HarlequinConnection

 Facebook.com/HarlequinBooks

 Twitter.com/HarlequinBooks

 Instagram.com/HarlequinBooks

 Pinterest.com/HarlequinBooks

ReaderService.com

ROMANCE WHEN YOU NEED IT

Love Harlequin romance?

DISCOVER.

Be the first to find out about promotions, news and exclusive content!

Facebook.com/HarlequinBooks

Twitter.com/HarlequinBooks

Instagram.com/HarlequinBooks

Pinterest.com/HarlequinBooks

ReaderService.com

EXPLORE.

Sign up for the Harlequin e-newsletter and download a free book from any series at **TryHarlequin.com.**

CONNECT.

Join our Harlequin community to share your thoughts and connect with other romance readers!
Facebook.com/groups/HarlequinConnection

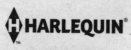

HARLEQUIN®

ROMANCE WHEN
YOU NEED IT

HSOCIAL2018